COSCOM
ENTERTAINMENT

# ZOMTROPOLIS

## A Record of Life in a Dead City

A.P. FUCHS

COSCOM ENTERTAINMENT
WINNIPEG

ISBN 978-1-927339-87-9



Published by Coscom Entertainment

Text set in Garamond
Printed and bound in the USA

Cover art by C.J. Hutchinson and Dark Riddle
Cover design by A.P. Fuchs

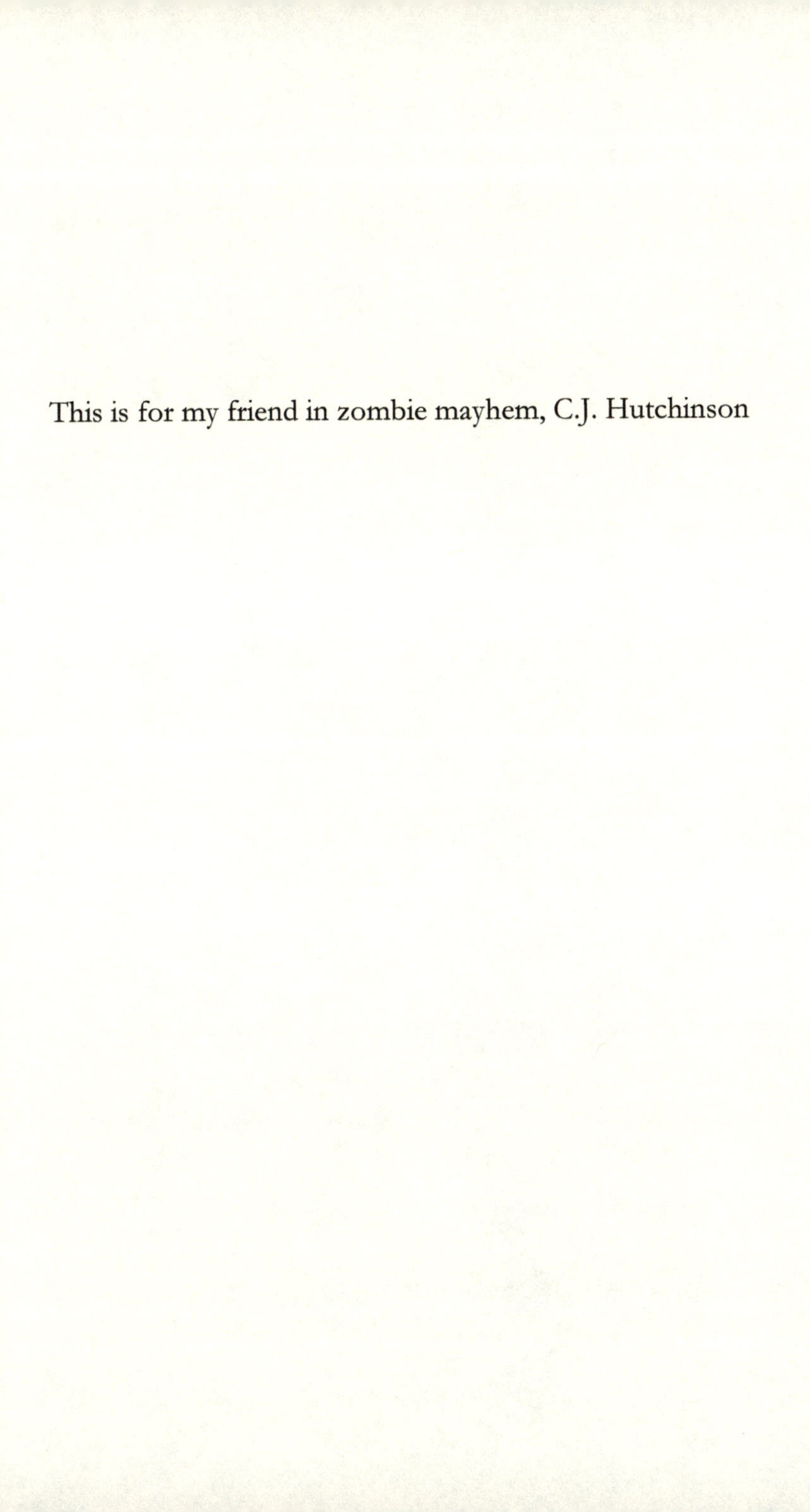

This is for my friend in zombie mayhem, C.J. Hutchinson

# ZOMTROPOLIS

### A Record of Life in a Dead City

# 1
# I Hate This

I'm so drunk right now I can hardly see straight. My head feels like it's in a mixer. My heart's somewhere in my gut, absent from my chest and just sitting there, boiling in stomach acid. And I feel every burn, every pinch.

It's a trippy thing when an ex-girlfriend comes back into your life. Except, in my case, Selena is dead.

Man, I hope I don't mess this up. Don't even know why I'm writing this. Catharsis, or whatever it's called, I guess. Maybe I'll go back later and check for typos. Maybe I won't.

Who cares.

It's getting to the point of being too much now, sitting here in this dingy apartment, waiting for the world to finally come to an end.

Oh, yeah. That already happened. Maybe I'm just waiting for my own world to come to an end. Wait, that happened already, too.

Stupid. Stupid. Stupid.

One would think that after sitting here in this stupid hole for the past two months I would have gotten used to having next to nothing to eat, next to nothing to drink, next to no sleep for nights on end.

Right, back to my ex. I guess you want to know what happened. Well, guess what? So do I. I mean, I can tell you *what* happened, give you the nitty-gritty about the night she waltzed back into my apartment and tried to rip a piece out of me again. Or maybe you want to hear about how after we first broke up and this girl messed me up so bad she landed me in the hospital on suicide watch? Wanna hear about that? I bet you do. If you didn't, you wouldn't be reading this.

Figures. People always love to hear about the downfalls of others, but when it comes to their own demise, they tend to back away.

I'm glad the human race is near dead. Probably just a few more weeks to go and it'll all be over. You. Me. And anyone else who's out there, hoping this thing would pass.

Sorry. Getting sidetracked. Hard to juggle two mind-benders at the same time. What's weird is that both of them have to do with death, dying, and more death.

Hang on. Got this bottle of tequila beside me. Need some. Say what you want but the stuff's great. Probably the only thing keeping me detached enough from reality that I'm even able to keep something of a brain together.

Booze never goes bad.

My ex. Man, why did she have to come back? And, boy, I tell you, she really *came back*. Lock, stock and two smoking barrels and all that.

Taking a shot. Hold on.

. . .

. . .

. . .

Done. Wait, here comes the pinch. Okay, I'm ready.

So . . . you really wanna know what went down about six hours ago?

Okay, I'll tell you.

Tomorrow.

# 2
# We're All Gonna Die

Look, I'm sorry about the other night. Probably wasn't a good idea to try and type drunk. I've gone back and cleaned up what I wrote. Got rid of the cursing and a host of profanities that I seemed to have made up on the spot. Not even sure what some of those mean. What's a "piss poking needle hammer," anyway?

You'd think that, at least these days, if someone is trying to connect—peacefully—with whomever's left on this planet, one would lay off being a foul mouth.

Okay. So, you're back to hear the story of my ex. I can give you the romance, all that "before" stuff. Or I can give you the horror, all that aftermath crap that everyone wants to hear but only once. After that it falls in the nobody-wants-to-hear-it category.

Wait. What's that? Right. I hear ya. Pretty standard, I guess. I knew what you were going to say even before you said it. You want the aftermath stuff.

Standard.

"Want the good news or the bad news?"

"Gimme the bad news first."

Weak. Typical human response.

Seriously, forgive me if I'm coming off a bit rough here but I've lost all faith in the human race. Even in what's left of it. We were never a good species to begin with and I don't care what you say, we're not a good species now. We've done too much damage over the years—yeah, since way back at the dawn of time—and now, it seems, it's finally caught up with us. Who or what has decided we all deserve a red-bottom spanking, I don't know, and right now it doesn't really matter. The real issue is: Where do we go from here? Onward, upward and all that stuff. Glass is half full. Lemons into lemonade.

Lemons. Had some with the tequila last night. Was already drunk when I pulled out my last one. Found out this morning when I woke up the thing was rotten because I spent the better part of the morning with my head in a bucket, puking up what's left of my guts and my heart.

See? I didn't lose focus. I brought up my heart for a reason. I nearly lost it yesterday. Nearly lost everything again and, after I logged off, took a razor to my wrist. Got a few scratches in and was about to make the big gash but passed out before I could. Us suicide-wannabes never finish what we start, do we?

So, you want to hear about Selena. Want to know why all this rambling before I really dive into it? I guess I'm holding off for a reason. Not for fear of having nothing to say and not because I don't know where to start. Things are a lot clearer today. Head feels like someone's stomping a boot on it, but inside—yeah, *inside*—things are pretty clear.

We're all gonna die.

# 3
# Geeky Gawker

Didn't mean to drop out on you yet again yesterday. Had something I needed to attend to (took me all day, actually), but I just needed to get it done before coming back on here. I promise. It won't happen again. Well, maybe. But if it does, I'm sure I'll have a really good reason as to why.

Okay, so let's get this thing going because I'm getting sick of beating around the bush, too.

Selena.

Oh man, it was all about her. Everything. Life. My heart. No one and nothing else mattered.

Though I'm a guy and, I suppose, compared to most, this was the most "un-guy" thing to do. I always knew, even from a young age, the type of girl that I wanted. I got glimpses of *her* throughout the school years, even way back starting in elementary. The way Jill smiled because Carl made a fart joke in class and even though it was unlady-like for her to think it was funny, she smiled anyway then covered her mouth when she couldn't hold back her laughter any longer. Or when Sammi came to school with a Superman comic, and me being the comic nut that I am suddenly took note, and this ugly girl became oh-so-attractive in my eyes because of that. Or how about the time when Amy came into our high school chemistry class wearing a suit and tie (nearly the same as the teacher's!) just so Mr. Finch could kick her out, and she'd get a few stares and laughs from her classmates. Man, I love a girl with an adventurous spirit. The list goes on and on. So many girls. So many qualities each one possessed that I so deeply desired, but so many other qualities they also possessed that eventually drove me away. I never told them I started to be attracted to them. Didn't want to girl hop. Maybe some of them. I don't know. Never had a girlfriend back in school. Not one. Was never liked all that much by those of the opposite sex.

But those girls . . . . Yeah. They each had something I wanted. Something I knew I liked. Stuff I connected with. Must have had a list of about thirty things going, everything from the superficial straight through to the important stuff like how my dream girl feels when it's raining outside. (Was she like me? Did she like to hide under a blanket, listen to the rain and suddenly become washed over in this utter feeling of safety, that the little pellets of water outside couldn't hurt her, that *nothing* could hurt her, here, in this dark place with nothing but the sound of the rain calming your soul?)

And along came Selena. She had everything. All of it. Not a one missing. If you could have only seen her the day I met her. Nothing out-of-this-world happened. I was at the art gallery. Me and a few other folks. Just minding my own business, checking out a wall of comic art when she came up beside me and asked me for the time. I remember turning to face her, see whose voice that was, a voice that, upon hearing it, sent a jolt up my spine and made my ears feel as if they were learning to hear clearly for the first time. She just stood there, looking at me with brown eyes so wide and so innocent that I forgot the question. I'm telling you, I couldn't breathe, couldn't move, couldn't do anything. All that I was just simply locked itself up inside, and I was lost in her.

Never, ever expected that happen.

She brushed back a lock of long, wavy brown hair back over her shoulder then hooked the lock on the other side behind her ear.

"Do you have the time?" she asked again.

I fumbled for my watch. Checked my right wrist instead of my left where it always was. "Um, yeah. It's 3:33."

She smiled, her lips soft around the edges. Not too big. Not too small. "Thanks." And she sidestepped over to the Wieringo piece beside me and lost herself in it.

My hands began to shake. Sweat lined the rears of my knees, and I think I was holding my breath because the next sound was a loud gasp. It was me.

She snapped around to face me, eyes wide. I completely startled her and even to this day I don't know what terrified her more: the loud gasp or the fact I had been standing there, staring at her for who knew how long like some geeky gawker who only saw beautiful women on the Internet.

"Sorry," I said and looked back at the piece that suddenly didn't seem worth looking at anymore. I thought about walking away, about going somewhere else in the gallery, anything to get my mind off her and free of the chance of looking like an idiot again. But I stayed there. Beside her. Not really looking at the art in front of me though pretending to. I just needed to be around her.

My heart bubbled inside. Butterflies let loose in my stomach. I lost my breath again and more than once had to wipe the sweat surfacing on my forehead.

This girl had gotten to me.

Selena moved about the gallery, going from one picture to another, all in order. I stayed beside her, pretending to do the same thing, superheroes and ink lines suddenly having lost all meaning to me.

By the time we were done, she waved me good-bye and made her way back downstairs. When she was about halfway down the winding steps, a weird squawk popped out of my throat and echoed throughout the place. The few others in the same gallery looked at me as if I was trying to be a bird or something and that the art gallery was hardly the place for that.

This time, Selena's eyes didn't go wide. Instead, they grew soft, expectant, asking me what I wanted.

"Do you want to go out for coffee?" I asked. Those weren't my exact words, but that was the gist of it.

And you know what?

She said yes.

# 4
# Everything

I know you had wanted the bad news first. The "aftermath" of me and Selena, as it were. And I honestly thought about getting right into it and unloading on you. I actually began typing but then stopped because, see, none of it would have made sense unless you understand what Selena was to me.

Everything.

After that day at the art gallery and after going for coffee at JavaJoe down the street, we at first just kept in touch via e-mail. Probably after, oh, eight or nine messages back and forth, I gave her my number just in case she wanted to call. Then the e-mails stopped, and there was nothing for a couple of weeks even after I sent two or three messages asking her how she was, what she was doing.

One day, the phone rang.

"Hello, is Marty there, please?"

She didn't even have to introduce herself. I knew that voice. It had been imprinted on my memory since she first spoke to me by that Wieringo Spider-Man pic.

"Hi, Selena," I said.

At first we just talked normal chit-chat, and she apologized for not e-mailing me back. Later that evening, when we met again at JavaJoe, she let it slip the reason she didn't message me back was because she was so nervous about giving me a call. She didn't want to go, as she put it, "the cheap route" and stick to e-mail and accidentally type the wrong thing.

It was then that I knew I had gotten to her, too.

We were at the coffee shop for four and a half hours and only left because the place was closing. I walked her home. It was a warm spring evening. Outside her apartment building, she asked me if I had a good time. I could tell by the way she said it she knew it was a cliché thing to ask but didn't know what else to say.

"I had a great time, Selena," I said softly.

She smiled as if those were the exact words she wanted to hear.

We stood so close together our toes were touching. I could feel every part of her, a warmth that emanated from her like steam from a bath. A warmth that came from within. She smelled of strawberries and vanilla, a smell that to this day I can still recall even though such smells are nowhere to be found.

I took her small hands in mine, gently squeezed her fingers and looked into her eyes. Selena leaned forward. I did, too. Our lips met, soft, gentle—perfect.

I had never kissed a girl before. But with Selena, it came so easily, so simple.

After, I took her right up to her front door and watched as she dug her keys out of her purse. When she pulled them out, she found the right one for the lock, stuck it in the door, turned it, but didn't go in. She looked at me, smiled, then jumped at me and wrapped her arms around my neck.

We kissed on that doorstep for an hour, totally oblivious to the time or where we were.

Only focused on each other.

It was then I fell for her.

# 5
# Nothing Lasts Forever

Didn't sleep last night. Couldn't. Wanted to. Even took about forty quick and short breaths to get myself lightheaded to help me drift away.

Nothing.

Just laid there atop unwashed sheets, thinking about Selena. She was alive. She was dead. Alive then dead. Alive then dead.

Memories swept me away last night, and I thought back to our time together.

Oh, I love her. I can't stop saying it. Can't stop thinking it. I never stopped, not even after everything ended, and I didn't see her for two years.

She gave me life and ruined it all at the same time. And now with her gone, there's not much point in going on, no other reason than to perhaps leave an account of one man's life so that whoever—if anybody—survives what's coming, they can at least have some kind of record of what things used to be like. Even if it was written by some love-struck loser who is so depressed right now he can hardly see the keyboard beyond the tears.

Going down memory lane and telling you about Selena is killing me, you know. These are memories I learned to suppress because they were getting too painful to recall. Every time I did, I wanted to hide under a blanket and pretend it was raining just so I could get away and retreat into myself. Maybe fall asleep and awake in a world that isn't dead anymore.

That's the thing about reality: try as we might, some

things just *are,* and there's absolutely *nothing* we can do about them. What makes it worse is not only are you depressed, trapped, and have lost all hope, you also have the sickly realization none of it can be changed.

None.

Forget what all those self-help gurus have told you. Sure, we can change our mind about some things, change our attitude and behavior and "start a new lifestyle." But you know what? That's all surface stuff. There is one thing that we can't change and that is our heart, the true and deep *who we are,* the part of us that simply *is* and no change of circumstance can alter it. And when who you are is tied so intricately with outward situations that are irreparable, hopelessness takes on a whole new meaning, and all you have left to do is either go through the motions and wait to die or just end it yourself and check out.

I've tried the former; failed on the latter. I don't know why I keep hanging on. I suppose it's because of Selena. Though she's dead and even though it was only her that could make life worth living again, Selena had one quality I never possessed but, I guess, am learning to have now: Dying hope.

"It's the most important thing in the world, Marty," she once told me. "You lose that, you lose everything."

Selena was willing to press on in all things even when it appeared there was no hope.

One night, after cuddling on my couch, holding each other, she told me her parents were killed four years earlier in a massive car wreck. She was an only child, just turned eighteen. Her folks didn't have life insurance and had a ton of debt. She had lost everything and had to sell the house, the car and everything inside except for some clothes just to pay off most of it. Her relatives lived either in the States or in other provinces and the distance over the years created a huge gap between her and her family. Some came for the funeral, the brothers, sisters, and the one living grandparent. The rest didn't. Most flew home the next day. A couple stayed on an extra day or two in a hotel.

Selena had been alone.

Once the house and assets had been liquidated, she was homeless. She had just graduated high school so didn't have a job. Her plans to go to university were squashed. For a month, she said, she lived on the street, bouncing around from shelter to shelter, if they had room. On the nights they didn't, she spent them beneath the Hellmouth Bridge, out of the elements, trying to sleep with hands over her ears to shut out the noise from the cars driving overhead.

At that point, she said, the only thing that kept her going was something her mom once told her: "It will pass. Everything does and nothing lasts forever."

Finally, she managed to get a job serving coffee to the late-night crowd at a coffee shop downtown that no longer exists. Slow but sure, she saved up enough for a damage deposit and first month's rent on an apartment. It was the same apartment I dropped her off at the night we first kissed.

Anytime throughout our relationship I talked about how bad things were, she always silenced me and reminded me that nothing lasts forever.

# 6
# How it Started

After I logged off from here last night, I sat for a long time on the worn-out sofa in my living room, counting the shadows on my wall. The power's out in my place. You might be wondering how I'm even typing this or getting this to you. I'm on a laptop and it's battery-operated. I also have a couple spares so once this one gives out, I'm still in good shape. The Internet connection? Wi-Fi. That stuff's still lingering on the air. The juice must still be on somewhere if I'm able to post this.

I think today's going to be a day of confessions. Or maybe tomorrow. Let's see how many words I can squeeze out before I can't take it any longer and need to take a break.

Let me tell you about the day everything changed.

It's when it all began, after all, the madness, the death.

The walking dead.

It started

# 7
# How it Started Again

Figures. Had something important to say and something went wrong.

Was about to tell you about what went down that day when all of the sudden my screen went black and the computer shut off. Tried turning it back on again. Wouldn't work. Wasn't 'til later—now—that I realized the battery connection must have loosened somehow and I lost power. Probably from the way I was holding it, balancing it on my lap.

Anyway, yeah, that day.

It was a day I *won't* forget.

It started off like any other. Well, mostly. I rolled out of bed around 10 (had a day off; used to be a donut delivery driver before things went to hell), hit the can then poured a bowl of Sugar Sharks Flakes and sat in front of the boob tube until I was done. I hate mid-morning programming. Nothing on but bad game shows and soaps, all streamed to you live. "Stories," as some call them. Yech.

When I was done my cereal, I dumped the bowl in the sink, went to the bedroom, got changed—white T-shirt and jeans—and for some reason wanted to double check my choice of attire so went to the window to see if the sun was shining. I hate light. Nowadays I wish I had more of it, but back then too much light always caused me headaches, so I kept my blinds shut most of the time. I opened them, looked outside and was pleased to see a T-shirt and jeans was a good choice. The sky was clear.

The sun was shining. A perfect day, something I needed because I was still hung up on Selena and, from what I heard, sunshine is good for your mood. You're supposed to get a half hour or so of it on your skin per day. Something about Vitamin D being a mood-lifter.

Anyway, I stared out my window, glancing down to the walkway leading up to my front door (I'm on the third floor). Phantoms of Selena and I taking our time walking toward the building filled the sidewalk, and if I let myself, I was able to lose myself so entirely in the moment it was like being there all over again. Her hand in mine, her head leaning on my shoulder, the sweet scent of her strawberry perfume filling me and making my head spin.

That's when things started to go dark. Just past the rooftops of the houses across the street, shadows rose on the horizon. At first I thought a simple spring rain was headed our way and figured I had maybe an hour or so before the rain would hit my area. But there were no clouds. Just shadow. Couldn't see what was causing it.

Then, just as suddenly, the shadow was gone and it was bright out again.

The thundering echo of two zipcars slamming into each other a skywalk-length from my place made me jump away from the glass. Did they fall out of the sky? I peered out, pressing my face against the glass, and caught a glimpse of the drivers hopping out of their vehicles in a mad panic—at first, seeming to check if the other was okay—then each quickly, still buzzing in the air via their anti-grav boots, holding out their hands palms up as if holding invisible barbells.

Another accident, this time an airbus speeding from the sky and slamming into a white Honda hovering above a curb. The airbus's passengers all ran out a minute later.

Then everything changed.

# 8
# Hiatus

You know what? Forget it. I was gonna do this big lead-in to what happened that day, get all dramatic, get your blood pumping and all the rest, but not anymore. That's the problem with the world I live in: Try and do something good and proper, and instead you get blindsided by some stupid, unexpected situation and BLAM! Totally screwed up.

Okay. I exaggerated on the unexpected part. Where I live, these days things are *very* expected.

There's a good reason why I haven't written in a while. I wanted to. Really wanted to.

Anyway . . .

Enough screwing around. Here's the deal: I logged onto my computer the day after I wrote you last and was about to type my first sentence when this stupid banging on glass jolted me from my thoughts. I live three floors above street level so I wasn't surprised when the windows to my apartment were free of anything that might be causing the disturbance. That means whatever it was was coming from downstairs. I didn't even have to leave my apartment to know what was going on.

I opened the window, peered down and, yup, sure enough, there they were.

Zombies.

A whole platoon of them.

Yes, they're real. I'm not joking. I may be a lot of things, but there's no way I'd try and slip you a fast one by stating the dead are walking when in reality they're not. That's not something you joke about. Ever.

The whole crew of them, with rotting faces, hands—even their clothes—are standing around the front of my building, banging against the glass as if they thought they could get in. They're not smart. They're not strong. They're stupid and slow. The only thing that makes them dangerous are: a) when there's a whole bunch of them; and b) when they're hungry.

The stories are true. The myth is real.

Zombies eat people.

So what did I do? I used to just get in my closet, shut the door and wait it out, fearing for my life. Nowadays, I'm more proactive. I can't stand the noise. That was one thing I hated about the "world of the living," by the way: the noise. The constant bickering of people, the racket of early-morning rush hour, the incessant blaring of tele-ads on those massive screens that are on nearly every street corner.

Ridiculous.

Anyway, there was no way I was going to let those dead guys down there ruin my peace and quiet, so I went to my utility closet and pulled out my secret weapon: an old Louisville Slugger coated in razor blades, each sharp tool jutting out from the wood like stakes. It was easy to make. Took me a while to hunt enough down blades and even longer to carve thin grooves in the wood for them, but after, dunk the bat in a bathtub filled with glue then insert each razor strong and sure. The thing's lethal.

It was just what I needed.

I threw on my boots, not paying any mind to the fact I was still in my boxers and white tank top, and stormed downstairs to face them.

At the bottom of the stairs, they stood on the other side of the locked dual-paned door, looking at me. One fat slab of a dead guy lunged forward, bounced off the glass, shook his head, then tried again. After bouncing off the second time, he seemed to get the idea, so just stood there as if waiting for me to open the door.

That's exactly what I did.

# 9
# Cutting Dead Flesh

Cutting dead flesh. There's nothing like it.

The guy looked at me just before the bat came down, his eyes doing a little dance that said, even despite his dead brain's lack of intellect, that he knew what was coming. The razors lodged themselves into the front of his skull, remained wedged in for a moment, then tore out on the follow-through as I yanked the bat downward. Blood spilled out from his forehead along with pieces of bone. The zombie staggered forward a step then fell on his face.

The others surrounding him didn't pay him any mind and came at me, arms outstretched, their palms open, seeming to be just itching to get hold of my shoulders, head, body, whatever.

I shoved my way through them, rounded them from behind, then took a chunk out of the back of the head of a short woman—about 5'2"—skull, hair and all. She fell. Same with the little boy who tried to gnaw a piece of my ankle like a dog on a soup bone.

The droning cries as the rest of them turned in their place then started toward me reminded me of the sound that seemed to be coming from my own heart as of late: one constantly aching and dripping with the memory of Selena and images of a better day.

But Selena was dead. She had to be. Most of the city was dead. I could have been the only one left, for all I knew.

Another dead guy lunged for me, his bulky shoulders

and thick arms displaying veins as thick as gardner snakes, which meant he must have hit the 'roids pretty hard in his former life. I slammed the baseball bat into his skin, the blades at its end slicing into the veins like a knife through sausage. Blood leeched from the veins. The wounds didn't faze him. I came back around and took the bat to the side of his head. His neck broke. When I pulled the bat free, blood and brain came oozing out. The guy dipped to the side then fell over.

The dead kept coming at me and for a brief moment, I considered letting them take me. If you've ever lived with depression, you'll know what I'm talking about. The apathy gets so strong sometimes that anything you're doing, anything you plan to do, anything you dream to do—all of it—just ceases to matter.

Even killing zombies.

Even surviving.

The moment passed and I caught a glimpse of my old self again, the one that wanted to live. Sure, it might have been what they call "survival instinct," or perhaps it was the adrenaline taking over. Regardless, I took out a few more undead before coming to the conclusion I wasn't going back upstairs anytime soon. The dead had blocked the entrance to my place. They'd stay there until I was either dead or one of them.

I only had one choice.

I had to run.

# 10
# Running

It didn't take long for my thighs to begin to burn. I was never an athlete by any stretch of the imagination, but I was never an out-of-shape loser either. I don't know what I weigh now, but last I checked I was sitting around 170 pounds, and at 6 feet, I have the advantage of long legs. Gaining distance between myself and those shamblers was the easy part. Maintaining that distance was another issue altogether.

I'm out of shape. Fine. I'll admit it, and ever since the city fell apart, navigating around its streets has become more of a challenge.

Lungs beginning to ache, baseball bat growing heavy, I rounded an alley some 10 blocks from my place. Perhaps there I could take a breather and wait things out. Nope. At the end of the alleyway, about five undead had their backs to me, and judging by the way they were hunched over and slightly bobbing up and down, they were feasting on something. Just seeing them made my jaw clench and my blood boil, and I instinctively tightened the grip on my bat. To club them one good. Man, what a thing. But they were five and I was one, and for some reason I was interested in living again.

So I ran elsewhere.

I just ran.

# 11
# The City

The city was called Comptropolis, the idea behind it being endless streets and towering buildings, a complex of wealth, opportunity, and freedom. The poor shmoes who designed this marvel of architecture had no idea what was coming. No one did. Now we got zombies, just like every other city in the world.

I've taken to calling this place "Zomtropolis" instead. Fitting, I think.

As I weaved my way down the motorwalks, dodging crashed hover-cars, airbuses wrapped around traffic poles and emergency vehicles scattered everywhere like a spilled bucket of tiny Hot Wheels—yeah, they still make those—I couldn't help but think back to how the city used to be before all this mess started.

There's not a single building in the city that's less than forty stories high. I remember aerial views on the weather network and how, from that high up, Comptropolis used to almost look like a computer's motherboard, all blocks and spires and shiny metal things. Hover-cars used to fly up and down the streets some ten feet from the ground, something vehicles had been doing for the past ten years or so. And though those were cool, it was the airbuses that people loved because airbuses actually flew-flew and the airspace above the city was theirs. Brilliant inventions, I think, and it cut the commute to work down to less than half.

At night, everything was Vegas, all lights, sounds, the laughter of people riding the motorwalks up and down the city streets, the honking of horns. Go, go, go. After the dawn of the Internet era, companies and investors had looked to new avenues of advertising once the Web got overcrowded with ads for nearly every webpage out there. So, taking an old idea, they billboarded everything—lampposts, traffic lights, hover-cars, airbuses, the overhead train, the sides of buildings. Two-way mirrors took on a whole new meaning as buildings were constructed with *two-way windows*, the interior side for looking out; the exterior for video and audio ads for whatever product was being pushed. I sometimes wondered where they got the money for this stuff. Billions were spent—and not just here, everywhere—and my only conclusion was that through some miracle those in charge just wanted to update and upgrade the globe.

So much for good ideas because now the buildings were dark, the two-way windows dead and without power, smashed and useless. I'm lucky I got intermittent power in my part of the city.

There was no one to buy anything anymore. (I, for one, am grateful money is a thing of the past; never was rich to begin with.)

The baseball bat suddenly weighed a ton and, unintentionally, I allowed its end to hit the ground. The jagged blades covering its end caught on the motorwalk and the bat jammed into the ground, its butt-end slamming into my stomach, sending me head over heels to the cement. Panting and lying on my back, dizziness sweeping my skull, the endless blue and white of the sky seeming something like a dream, I considered staying there and resting up before moving on.

But the groans that began to materialize on the air told me I'd better not.

# 12
# Time = Meaningless

One of the things I've noticed about the nature of time ever since the zombies came was that it no longer held any meaning. Living alone with only my back to watch out for had set me on a *very* open schedule. Day and night, though still separated by blue and black skies, were a non-issue. I slept when I was tired. Stayed awake when I wasn't. No job to go to anymore. The boss and my co-workers were either dead or walking around dead. People took what they wanted *when* they wanted, and those of us still alive, it seemed, preferred indoor life.

But time also had a new meaning when around the undead. See, movies and books and video games prepared us for it—kinda—helped us get lost in the moments when the dead came around and tried to kill you or the heroes in the stories. Only one habit was practiced when you watched on your projecto-screen the dead coming for the living: Survival. It didn't matter how long it took or which way it took you.

Same thing happened laying there on that sidewalk. I heard their low, raspy moans. I saw the sky above. My thoughts raced and yet I could think through each one clearly: get up and run; get up and fight; lie there and die; lie there, fight a little, then die some strange heroic death after one last stand.

So what did I choose?

I got up and fought.

Getting to my feet was the easy part; the adrenaline pumping through my system took care of any effort getting up that quickly might have taken under normal circumstances. My head swooned a touch, my only thought locating my bat. There it was, off to the side a few feet, laying there like a sword begging to be plucked from a stone. I grabbed hold of the handle and felt its power surge through me.

Eyes level, I saw the dead approaching, a whole group of them, at least a dozen, the mass of dead flesh, gray and decayed stepping steadily toward me, their eyes bloodshot and dreamy, transfixed on me, their next meal.

I took a few steps back as I leveled the bat. Then I set my feet shoulder-width apart and wound up like a star hitter waiting for the pitch.

Closer. The dead came forward.

When the first one—a burly old broad with shoulder-length, dust-covered blonde hair—reached for me, I swung the bat hard and swift into the side of her head. Her neck snapped, the flesh along one side tearing from the impact. I came up from the other side, cracked her skull, ripping the blades through her flesh, and watched her tumble to the side as blood leaked from her ears.

An old man came in from the left and tried to grab me with his no-longer-functioning robo-arm. I brought the bat down on the apparatus just as a little kid who appeared about eight years old wrapped his arms around my waist and tried to take a chunk out of my stomach. I brought the butt-end of the Louisville down into the top of his head, shoved him away, then drove the bat between his legs like that Tiger Woods guy from decades ago.

More zombies appeared. Lots more, coming in from each side, making their way around the smashed hover-cars crowding the street.

I got out of there.

The dead tried to run after me, most of them falling

over as they suddenly tried to propel their legs faster than they could handle. Some stumbled a few steps then started walking regular pace, seeming to think they'd still be able to catch up with me. Nothing doing.

I ran home.

# 13
# Home Again

So I'm sitting here, writing all this stuff out for you, my body still lined with a sticky film of sweat about an hour after all this occurred. I can't even remember why I went outside to begin with.

Wait. Let me check.

Right. Needed some peace and quiet so decided to bust some heads. Got a little carried away, I guess.

My hands are sore, achy, and if I stop and just let them *sit* for a sec, I can still feel the flesh and bone tingling from smacking those zombies with the slugger.

It feels good.

Before, just as I was approaching my apartment, I was partly delighted yet disappointed to see only a handful of the dead standing outside my building. Despite how tired I was, I wanted to take out a few more.

Overpowering another life, yeah, that's what it was about. More like overpowering an *unlife*—but still. You do it once, you're left in a state of shock, wondering what just went down and if it's even possible for you to kill someone else. Do it again, it suddenly becomes about survival and self-defense. Do it a third time and it becomes a game because you realize what you're killing isn't a person anymore, and whoever they were had checked out a long time ago and all that was left was a skin-and-bones piñata without the candy inside.

The five that still hung around my building were taken care of easily enough. I drove the end of the bat pretty good into the face of one and sliced the neck of another so much her trachea spilled out. The other three came at me all at once, slow and clumsy, and each one was dropped with a cracked skull. I had to step around the brains to get back in the front door.

And now I'm here, still covered in blood, stinky and sweaty, the memory of being out there killing zombies something that happened to someone else yet at the fore of my mind all the same.

. . .

. . .

This is the first time for me to write anything, I mean *really* write something long and, hopefully, with meaning, so I just went back to the first entry and skimmed it over. I was going to tell you about what happened "six hours ago." Guess it's not six anymore. Too much has happened since. Let's just call that time period "before" and call it good.

Let me tell you about what happened *before.*

Selena. She was my *before.* Even before I met her, she was my *before.* I've always known her, saw her in different people (as you know) until I met her for real one day. You also know the overview of it not working out and all the rest.

But there's another *before* you need to know about.

One involving Selena, a zombie, me, and a whole lot of blood.

# 14
# Before

I couldn't take it anymore. The wondering.

I had to know if Selena was alive.

Though the world got screwed up a long time before, *not knowing* was killing me.

I did the math: everyone dead equaled she was dead, too.

Still didn't compute. That's the funny thing about hope. No matter how bleak the circumstances, no matter how unlikely things would work out, it still nagged at you, telling you that somehow, some way, some *when* everything would be all right.

I got online, did some searches, feeling something like a super spy able to discover whatever I wanted at the touch of a button.

See, nowadays everybody's plugged into the Net. Most people are users; the only ones who aren't are those who live on the streets. Communication was everything before the dead rose. Still is now—if you could find somebody to talk to. Have a job? There's a trail somewhere in Cyberspace. Have money? Your transactions are wired into the Net, too. Like movies? Same deal. All rentals are done on-line. No more going to the video store for us folks who like vintage places, but even if you do shop at the few left, those rentals are still tracked via the store's Website.

I digress.

Finding Selena's new address didn't take long, even with my addled brain. I must have stood there for a half hour in front of my screen just thinking about what I was going to do. See, Selena didn't want to have anything to do with me. Long story there, but let's just say I didn't handle the break up very well. Had a thing for trying to contact her after the fact even after being repeatedly told the show was over.

But this was different. It wasn't every day the world ended. I figured she'd cut me some grace and let the past be the past.

If I found her, that was.

When I finally went outside, it was evening, the cool air just setting in, the silence of a dead city almost soothing to the nerves (if I made an effort to not think about what was out there).

I began walking. For every zombie I saw, I made sure I had ample time to either hide or take a different route. It caused the walk to Selena's to take forever. I got there, however, some two hours after I left (I think). She lived in a high-rise called Sweet Iris, the building's name making zero sense (as did a lot of the things named in Comptropolis). I didn't know how long she had lived there. It had been awhile since we last spoke. It didn't matter.

Sweet Iris looked to be about fifty stories tall. Her suite number was 4912, so I assumed that meant the forty-ninth floor.

The front door, all glass, had been smashed a long time ago. I went in, the stench of rotting flesh thick on the air. I stepped back outside and breathed in deep and readied myself to get back in there and "take it like a man."

Once back inside, I kept taking big gulps of air, holding it, as I went further in, thinking the less I breathed the better off I would be. Then I realized that by holding the air in, I was allowing my lungs ample time to fully absorb whatever microscopic organisms were in the air. Even diseased.

Breathing normal, I finished crossing the expansive lobby, one lined with wilting trees and a no-longer-running stream with gold fish floating belly-up on its surface. Must have been nice back in its heyday.

The elevators were dead, and the thought of climbing forty-nine floors made my stomach do a flip.

Then I remembered it was for Selena.

It was always about Selena.

———

I nearly died by the time I finally reached her door. Panting, heart rapping inside my chest, I had to put a hand against the doorframe to deal with my dizzy head and the stitch in my side.

Selena's door.

I've been here a million times before—not at this new place, but Selena's *door*—both when I was with her and in my mind ever since. This door was a gateway to a world of love, pleasure and the infilling of something that only happens when you meet the one person you're sure you're destined to be with forever.

The feeling of her safety was there, overwhelming me, and for a moment I forgot about the creatures lurking outside and how the rest of the world was dead.

Then reality came back and there I was, ready to find my girl.

I kicked down the door.

Selena's apartment was rank, the funk of death immediately bringing bile up to the back of my throat.

The white walls and ivory-colored doors that lined the

foyer were off-yellow, as if caked in nicotine.

I closed the door behind me and checked the light switch, just in case. No power. I inadvertently glanced back at the door and felt tears well up in my eyes at what I saw: blood, dark smears of the stuff all up and down it as if Selena had tried to beat down the door and busted her hands open in the process. Why she hadn't used the handle, I didn't know, unless—

Then it hit me.

She couldn't escape. Something or someone stopped her.

Movement behind me.

I spun around, Louisville ready, just itching to plow it into the skull of the monster that took my sweet girl.

The floor was coated in blood, black and dried.

Slowly, I stepped forward, gently placing one foot in front of the other as lightly as I could so as not to make a sound. Too late. The dried blood on the wooden floor cracked as I walked on it.

I passed the kitchen on the right, the one where we cooked our first-anniversary meal together. No, wait, that was the other place. Heart aching and throat dry, I pressed on. The living room was next and it was just behind the ornate swinging door in front of me.

I thought about getting out of there, about running for safety.

But I had to know.

I gently pushed open the door.

That's when she charged me.

# 15
# Before, Part II

The zombie came, arms outstretched, reaching for my neck and shoulders. I stepped to the side; she narrowly missed me. The zombie had its back to me but before I could raise the bat, long, matted brown hair swirled around and a pair of yellow teeth burst forth from a pair lips along with a terrible hiss. Those eyes, sunken and dead, looked at me with such hunger that I couldn't believe Selena would—Selena . . . Selena . . . it wasn't Selena.

The zombie grabbed hold of me, locking its arms around my waist. My own arms were free. I dropped the bat on purpose and shot out my hands and held back the dead girl's head so her snapping jaw wouldn't take a bite out of my face. I had to know for sure. The girl's skin was bumpy and boiled, gray and lifeless. Chipped, yellowed teeth snapped up and down in front of a shriveled tongue. Vacant eyes kept staring straight ahead, just past me, as if seeing something that wasn't there. It just kept snapping its mouth open and closed and open and closed and . . . those eyes.

They weren't brown.

They were blue—faded—but blue.

Thank God.

I shoved the dead girl away from me, quickly crouched down, picked up the Louisville, then let her have it across the skull. The razors along the bat's weighted end lodged themselves into her head. I ripped them clean out, dragging along bits of flesh and bone with it. Syrupy blood splashed against the floor. The zombie teetered to the side. I came down on her head with the bat again. She fell. I stepped on top of her stomach and plowed the slugger into her face at least twenty times.

She made me think she was Selena.

After her face and head were good and gone and were nothing more than a stringy mess of skin, blood, and bone, I finally stepped off her and moved to the side.

Then I heard something coming from the direction of the bedroom.

I kicked what was left of the dead girl's head just for good measure.

She made me think she was Selena.

She made me think . . .

That sound again.

The bedroom.

I moved toward it.

Selena's bedroom was just down the hallway, the room on the right just before the bathroom at the end. I've been down that hallway hundreds of times before— no, wait, that was the other place—and there was one time in particular that I'll always remember. More on that in a second.

The Louisville unexpectedly grew heavy, my heart pounding knowing what I might find. The hallway's white walls seemed oddly out of place all of a sudden, the white an awful contrast to the dark world Comptropolis now found itself in never mind the darkness in my own heart telling me I didn't belong in such a bright a place as this.

I hoisted up the bat shoulder height and stood in front of the bedroom door. Inside, dull thunks echoed; at first just one then a whole series of them. They stopped then resumed. Stopped then resumed. Then kept on going, each thunk nearly matching the frantic beating of my own heart. It took a moment for me to realize tears had formed at the corners of my eyes. I thought I was already all cried out over her. Now . . .

My breathing sped up and no matter how hard I tried to slow it down, I couldn't. Throat dry, I clenched the bat, reached out—and opened the door.

*Thunk, thunk, thunk. Thunk, thunk, thunk.*

Across from me, in between a pink-quilted bed high enough above the ground for a princess and an ornate dresser up against the wall beneath the window, was a girl who I'd recognize anywhere, back turned to me, repeatedly walking into the wall, her head smacking against it as if trying to beat out black and tormenting thoughts.

Selena.

She wore black pants, a gray sweater a couple sizes too big, no shoes. Her wavy brown hair hung loose halfway down her back.

My arms ached to reach out and hold her.

*Thunk, thunk, thunk.*

I wanted to speak, to get her attention. My voice caught in my throat, and the words didn't come.

I stepped in further, each foot dragging a dumbbell.

*Thunk, thunk, thunk.*

"Se—Selena . . ." I barely managed.

*Thunk, thunk, thunk.*

I went closer, about ten feet away.

"It's me. Marty. Are you—" My voice caught again. I cleared my throat. "Are you—" I wanted to ask if she was okay but something inside me said that if I asked that, that when I saw her it would hurt even more.

Only a few feet behind her now, my bat still raised.

She kept pounding her head against the wall.

"Selena . . ." I reached out and touched her shoulder.

Selena kept hitting her head.

I tried again, this time pulling a bit on her right shoulder to help turn her around.

She did.

She was dead.

Her gaunt skin was like skim milk, her brown eyes pale and vacant, almost chalk-like. Dry, cracked lips that hadn't seen a drink in who knew how long grinned then displayed yellow teeth just like the other girl.

My arms dropped, the bat suddenly too heavy for me to carry. I still held onto it, though I couldn't bring it up in between us when she lunged at me. A dull *thump* boomed inside my skull and the back of my head lit up in dry pain. It took a second to realize I was on the carpet, Selena on top of me, seeming to weigh twice as much as she did when she was alive though no extra weight showed.

Growling, her mouth went immediately to my neck. I jerked my head to the side, bought a few inches, then let go of the bat and pulled my hands up between us and pushed her off. Rolling over, I scrambled to my feet, Selena somewhere behind me. Running to the opposite side of the room near a closet, I firmly planted my feet, raised my fists and got ready. She darted toward me, low, guttural groans dripping from her mouth like drool. She didn't recognize me or care who I was.

The realization almost paralyzed me then, her not caring. Felt too much like how she treated me after we'd finished dating.

My bat was on the other side of her.

She latched onto me with both hands, her grip hard and firm, squeezing the life out of the muscles just beside my neck. On instinct, I shot my fist out, punching her in the chest, the force strong enough to cause her body to bend at the waist. She straightened in no time then came in again, this time forcing me into her. I went with this, shooting my weight forward, knocking her to the ground so this time I was on top. Of all things to think or feel or notice, when I drew my hands in between her arms to break her hold on my neck, it reminded me of the time she had once put her arms around me, drawing me in for a kiss. I had similarly reached in between her arms, gently pulled them down then ran my hands across her cheeks and brought her face close to mine. Our lips locked, tongues searching the other's, nothing but passion and love.

A kiss of need.

Now, I put my hands to her face again, this time gripped her hard, my fingers close to her ears, my thumbs on her cheekbones. I bent my arms at the elbow then shot them straight out, slamming the back of her head against the floor.

I did it again, this second time fazing her.

I got off her and ran for my bat. When my fingers wrapped around the wooden handle, it was like coming home. Movement behind me. Spinning around, I was greeted by a blur of brown hair and gray material. I cracked the bat across her face. Her body reeled to the side. One giant step closer and I brought it down on the back of her skull. Her neck cracked. She dropped to her hands and knees.

Whatever tenderness for her that was in my heart vanished and was replaced with the life-giving breath of rage.

"You took everything from me!" I screamed.

The bat came down, plowing once more into her skull. Her body dropped by my feet, prone, face down. I got on my knees, rolled her over, her dead eyes now bloodshot, her face a mish mash of ripped flesh and blood.

"I loved you and you destroyed my life! I hate you! I hate you!" And I brought the butt end of the bat down into her nose, crushing it.

Selena coughed, threw up blood, then tried to attack me, though the attempt was feeble.

"How could you!" I shrieked. "How could you!"

Nothing but low groans escaped her lips.

She didn't hear me.

She didn't care.

# 16
# Watersheds

What's sick about all this is that my whole life boils down to Selena. There's my life before her and my life after. No in between or some kind of transition period or years of maturing or anything that goes with growing up. I suppose every life, in the end, has some kind of watershed. Selena was mine.

Just wish it wasn't so painful.

I'm home now, writing this (obviously), thinking that perhaps a new watershed has presented itself.

Madness.

My new turning point.

I had beat whatever was left of life out of Selena.

Scratch that.

I had beat whatever was left of *death* out of Selena and . . . and killed her.

I . . . killed her.

Can't finish this now.

Later.

# 17
# Watersheds (redo)

Like I said, my life changed because of one girl. Now, it seems, it's changing again thanks to the world's descent into chaos and the living dead.

In that bedroom, sitting next to her body, covered in blood, I didn't cry. Most people would. Anyone who kills the one they love would bawl 'til their eyes bled. But I do remember the buzzing inside my head, my brain feeling like it was soaked with alcohol and the lightheadedness that goes with being stoned.

I sat there, her head in my lap, my hands stroking her hair over what was left of her skull after I had dismantled it with the Louisville. Glancing around the room—this foreign bedroom yet somehow familiar; probably because it was hers—I remembered that particular time I hinted at earlier.

It was the time she and I first made love.

Both of us had been raised proper, the idea being not to have sex before marriage. Believe me, many nights after long make out sessions we fought with everything we had not to give in and go one or ten steps further. In hindsight—and perhaps this is only the part of me my parents raised talking—I'm glad we abstained as long as we did because the night we did first get a glimpse into each other worlds was so powerful, I'm sure our abstinence played a huge part in it.

That hallway, the two of us walking down it hand-in-hand, each breathing choppy due to racing and apprehensive hearts, was like a tunnel to a new world where discovery awaited and rebirth was just around the corner.

We went into the bathroom first, Selena turning on the shower, the room suddenly filling with the moist warmth of steam and the security that goes with it.

I was in a regular T-shirt and jeans that night. She wore jeans, too, and an oversized white sweatshirt from the high school she went to.

When she turned toward me after testing the water, she smiled, brown eyes glowing, both of us scared and excited.

We didn't really plan this per se, but more so came up with the idea while watching television in her living room, ignoring what was on and instead focusing on each other. One didn't even have to tell the other that we were going to take the next step. We both just kind of knew. I looked at her, she looked at me, and we both nodded at the same time.

The shower part was her idea. Thought it might smooth any awkwardness that might come later.

She was right because as we slowly undressed and stole glances at the other as each piece of clothing was taken away, it felt almost natural, as if her and I had done this a hundred times before.

Once we were naked, we immediately held each other as if in an indirect effort to conceal ourselves from the others' eyes.

We went into the shower, kissing most of the time, talking at others, then went to her bedroom, each wrapped in a towel. When we got to her bed, we pulled the covers back together then, as a game, counted to three and ripped our towels away.

All that followed changed our relationship.

Changed my life.

Changed hers.
Changed everything.

———

I need to stop. I know you might be disappointed that I didn't get into detail about what happened in the bedroom or anything that happened many times after that, but to be honest, all physical pleasure aside, sex wasn't about the pleasure for us anyway. Yes, it was there, but the connecting, the falling deep into someone else, the revelation of that private side of them that was only reserved for one other was the cornerstone of our physical relationship.

It was about love.

Making love.

Making it real.

Making it last.

And it did last.

Sure, things ended badly, but the love part never did. At least on my end. That's why I can't begin to describe to you what it was like killing Selena because, I think, by having done that, I killed myself, too, the part that understood what it was doing despite the desperate survival instinct that took over, despite the rage and need for revenge for her ripping my heart out and ruining my life.

It was that love that was my watershed.

It was her death that was my watershed, too.

It was—

Um . . . okay. There's a knock at my door or at least what sounded like one.

Hang on.

Let me check.

Couldn't be a zombie. Zombies don't . . .

. . .

. . .

I dropped my bat on my foot.
I'm telling you now in case something happens.
I looked through the peephole.
It was Selena.

# 18
# Selena

I'm not ready for this.

Selena's supposed to be dead, and not just dead, but *undead.*

I would know.

I killed her.

Yet there she was, human, on the other side of my door. Through the fisheye lens of the peephole, there doesn't seem to be a mark on her face. I can't see the rest of her body, only a dark blur beneath the neck. I hope the rest of her is all right, but it wouldn't surprise me in the least if I've finally lost it and all this is an illusion, some kind of wishful thinking that is manifesting before my eyes.

I can scarcely breathe. A dead weight is on my toe. I kick it away and hear my baseball bat roll awkwardly to the side, one of the pieces of razors glued to it breaking as it moves across the floor.

Hand shaking, one eye still glued to the peephole, I slowly unlocked the door, felt my way up the doorframe to the chain, unhooked it.

She stood there on the other side, brown eyes wide and uncertain, a million thoughts clearly racing behind them.

Something moves in the peephole, small, delicate, flesh-toned.

*Knock, knock.* Then again, only louder.

"Yeah," I said, but my voice is only a whisper.

Any strength I had within was gone and I found

myself on the floor, a sharp pain racing up my tailbone and into my lower back.

"Marty?" I hear through the door. "Is that you? Please, let it be."

For the longest time I would have given anything to hear her call my name again and now that it's finally happening, I wish she was gone.

Like I said, I'm not ready for this.

Heart speeding, pulsing in my throat and thumping through every vein in my body, I braced myself against the door and, using it for leverage, slowly pulled myself up.

"I'm here," I said. Same thing. My voice was a whisper.

Fingers trembling, I turned the door knob and pulled, the door weighing a thousand pounds and then some. It took two hands to pry it open.

Still leaning against it, I took in the sight before me. My heart was empty, hollow, void of feeling and life.

Selena stood a couple feet from the door, barefoot, wearing nothing but a grubby garbage bag that hung on her like a dress from the dark.

"You're alive," I rasped.

"Marty, I need to come in," she said.

We stood there in silence, my mind void of thought. This was Selena, the girl from long ago and the one who changed everything for me. She was here, alive, at my door in a world of zombies.

"Then who'd I kill?"

I barely mouthed the words but she must have heard them because she said, "Who'd you kill?"

*I killed you,* I thought. *I beat your brains out and unloaded on you all my hate and pain and—* "Come in."

I moved from the door and she stepped into my

apartment.

*Crnch.*

Selena shrieked, dropped to the floor and cradled her foot. I knelt down beside her.

She had stepped on that razor blade that had broken off the bat.

———

There was only one way to handle this: pretend she wasn't her and clean her up. After that, I could figure things out. If living in a world filled with the undead had taught me anything, it was that sometimes you had to stop feeling, stop caring, stop being what it meant to be human and just *go through the motions.* Survival was like that whether physical or otherwise.

I always hated "otherwise."

Selena was now sitting on my couch, me kneeling before her, her foot in my lap. I ignored how good it felt to hold her heel in my hand and suppressed the memory of the time I kissed every inch of her body, starting with her feet. I gently removed the razor with a pair of tweezers then pressed hard against the wound with a cloth. She winced. I told her it was going to be okay. A moment later she reached down and her hands replaced mine. Again I had to fight the resurgence of memory when her soft hands trailed against my own.

I stood, took several steps back, and began pacing.

It was silent for a long time, and I wasn't sure if it was because she was too busy attending to her foot or if it was because silence was what happened every time you ran into an ex.

But this wasn't "running in." She had come here intentionally.

"Everybody's dead," she said.

I stopped pacing. "I know."

"Except me and you."

"You don't know that."

"Yes, I do."

"You can't."

"I do."

"No, you can't," I said firmly.

"The city's empty, Marty."

"Some might be indoors, like us. Besides" —I strolled over to my window and looked down onto the street— "*they're* out there."

"I know. I saw a million of them on the way over here." I turned to face her. She glanced up from her foot. "I don't even know how I made it here without them touching me."

"Where were you?"

"Home."

The last thing that I wanted was to come across as a creepy ex-boyfriend even though I was one hundred percent certain that was how she viewed me, and she was only here because she had nowhere else to go, and it was better to be with someone than no one at all, but I had to tell her. "Selena, I was just at your place."

Her eyes went wide.

"Yeah, for real. I was there. I came to see you. I had to see you." The last bit obviously made her uncomfortable because after I said it she immediately went back to tending to her foot.

"Okay, fine," I said. "Regardless, I was there. There were zombies in your apartment. You weren't. I checked the whole place, so unless you were hiding somewhere over there that I don't know about and didn't bother even peeking to see what the commotion was about, you need to tell me where you've been and why only now you decided to come see me."

She looked up from her foot but not at me. "Okay, I'll tell you. Just listen and believe whatever you want. I was home. I heard the dead, the groans, the biting of flesh. I don't remember you being there or seeing you, and it may just be shock right now so I'm forgetting something, but I remember walking and walking." Tears welled up in her eyes. "Wait." She glanced down at the garbage bag covering her. "Oh no." She sniffled. She glanced up at me, tears dripping down her cheeks. "I have lost something or something happened or . . ."

I came over to her, sat beside her, and put a hand on her shoulder. She pulled away.

"Sorry," I said.

"No, it's just that I was walking, and I don't know for how long then I looked down on myself and . . . and I wasn't wearing anything. Nothing. I—" She paused and took a deep breath. "I don't know how I lost my clothes or if one of those things tore them off or what, but anyway I found this" —she touched the garbage bag— "put it on and realized I was close to your place." She turned away and shame coated her voice. "I didn't want to come."

I took a deep breath. "I understand."

"Sorry."

"You need to get cleaned up. I'll give you something to wear. We'll take it slow and figure things out. Just know that we're safe for now, okay?"

"Thanks," she whispered.

I left the room and headed to my bedroom. Once inside, I leaned against the wall. She didn't want to come here and only did out of desperation.

I wished I knew what happened to her.

# 19
# Now, with Selena Here

Selena's sleeping on my couch as I type this. I gave her a pair of underwear, socks, brown sweatpants, and a green sweatshirt. They should keep her warm enough and provide some sense of security. I had wanted to rest, too, but I'm afraid that if I fall asleep, I'll awake later and she'll be gone.

I can't let that happen despite what I did to her—to that zombie—earlier. I don't know who that creature was back in her apartment, but obviously it wasn't her.

The things I said.

The thing I did.

I'm pathetic.

The main question is: What now? What does this mean, her and I reconnecting? I can't make too much of it. Not with the city the way it is. So far as I know, we're safe here. I got some water, some food, clothing, the basics. Eventually that stuff is going to run out, and we're going to have to get more if we want to survive. Before, I didn't really care all that much about survival. The original plan was to hang out as much as I could and then if one of those monsters devoured me or I simply died of starvation or dehydration, I was fine with it.

Now, with Selena here, suddenly everything's changed.

Selena's good at that: changing things.

I'm going to wait for her to wake up. When she does, the first thing we need to do is get some stuff settled. I'll remind her that our survival is at stake.

Let's just hope it doesn't turn into an argument.

Let's just hope she doesn't storm out of here and get herself killed.

# 20
# Selena's Dream

Selena awoke screaming. I was in the next room about to write you something else, but instead was jolted from the first few sentences by Selena's shrieks and her kicking at the couch. I ran into the room. She was on her back, arms flailing, legs coming down on the worn couch cushions heels first. I've seen her sleep before. Back when we were dating, she told me about the occasional nightmare, but not once did she talk about freaking out like she was doing on my couch just now.

Her eyes were closed.

I called her name.

She kept screaming, kept kicking.

I called her name again. Nothing. Just hysterics.

I thought about going over to her and putting a hand on her shoulder and giving her a little shake.

I didn't.

Didn't want her to lash out at me and, besides, I figured, if she was flipping out this bad on her own, what was a little shake by me going to do? It was kind of like watching an epileptic having a seizure: the most you could do was wait it out and make sure they didn't hurt themselves in the process.

Finally, after several long minutes, her screaming and flailing ceased. She opened her eyes, sat up abruptly, face shiny with sweat, and tried to catch her breath.

I waited a few moments before saying anything. "You okay?"

Still panting, she looked at me. "I saw them, Marty. I saw *them*. So real. So flippin'—" She coughed. It was a deep cough, one loaded with phlegm. She winced as she tried to stifle another one.

"I'll get you some water," I said and hit the kitchen. When I came back and handed her the glass—water jugs are still around, for those wondering; water doesn't suddenly disappear when the world goes down; don't trust the movies—she held it for a while before taking a sip. Once done, she set the glass down on the coffee table and kept looking around the living room as if expecting a zombie to jump out at her at any moment.

"We're safe here," I said. "We're up high. Everything's locked. It's okay."

"It's not that," she said. "Well, it is. The dream, Marty. So real. Vivid. Every face. Every sound. Every smell. Never had smell in a dream before."

Come to think of it, she had a point. I don't remember ever smelling anything in my dreams either.

"Want to talk about it?" I asked.

Back when she and I were together, we were real good at confiding secrets, talking all night and overloading each other with information. It seemed she remembered that because a calm came over her face, and the way she looked at me indicated she trusted me enough to spill her guts.

I sat beside her and listened.

"I was in a hallway," she said. "Dark. The walls were silver. I knew that because there was the occasional bit of light that seeped into the hallway from the rooms that ran off it and illuminated the wall enough to see they were silver. You know, tinfoil-like, but not crinkled. The floors were silver, too. Same with the ceilings. I remember thinking in the dream that I wanted to find a light switch so I could see the light shimmer off the walls. It'd be like being inside a diamond.

"So that's what I did: looked for a light switch.

"The air smelled like lemon cleaner, but also like compost. Real weird combination. As I went down the hallway, I heard footsteps behind me. I stopped, turned around and, far away at the opposite end, was a human-like shadow. I could tell by its posture that it was female and that it was dead.

"It started moving toward me."

She took a deep breath. I already felt my heartbeat double with apprehension.

"I turned and picked up my pace," Selena said. "The undead woman's footsteps got closer together, and I didn't have to look back to know it was stumbling toward me with everything it had. I tried running, but no matter how hard I dug in, I still couldn't get past going at a walking pace.

"Moans filled the hallway. Low, hollow moans that at first didn't sound like it would come from the undead. Then groans started and the growls. That one coming up at me from behind wasn't alone. The hallway I was in just kept going. Silver walls all looking the same, no sense of distance or goal at the end.

"I glanced over my shoulder. A pack of female zombies were, like, twenty feet behind, if that. Their grubby hands were already reaching out for me. Dark hair, their mouths open, all naked. What was bizarre was their pale skin didn't appear all that decayed, from what I could see. Didn't matter, though. That gray was disgusting. So lifeless, so wan and empty of blood. Makes me shudder just thinking about it. I could smell them, like cooking oil left on the stove hours too long after a deep fry.

"My thighs burned. I kept running anyway until it was like my legs were filled with sand and every step forward was like lugging tree stumps for feet.

"The undead moaned and growled.

"Dead hands grabbed my shoulders and pulled me back. I fell and hit the floor. I remember looking at the silver ceiling beyond their dead faces, the silver reflecting the scene below. There were over a dozen of them now, all naked and dead and crowding over me trying to get a piece. A pair of hands reached down and tugged at my clothes. I wore a hospital gown. They tore that off then sharp dirty fingernails poked their way into my skin, through the flesh and in between the bones of my ribcage. They just kept digging. Soon they were in far enough they were able to curl the ends of their fingers around those bones and they started to pull.

"I howled, but not from pain. I just howled because I thought that was what I was supposed to do.

"Blood sprayed everywhere. Bones snapped. They pulled my ribs away from my body, my flesh hanging off the bones like tattered rags. The undead women brought the bones to their lips and sucked the meat off before chewing on the bones themselves.

"I glanced at my chest and saw nothing but a wet, black bowl spurting blood and bubbling over with internal organs. They ripped my lungs from my body. I stopped breathing. My stomach, guts, liver, kidneys— everything—they tore free and brought the red and dripping chunks of meat to their mouths. Blood dripped from their faces and splashed onto my own. I wanted to scream but, again, I couldn't breathe. All I could do was scream inside my head. I tried kicking and using my arms to push them away but I couldn't move.

"The wet sounds of them eating . . . I can still hear them now. Those sounds." She pressed her palms to her chest and stomach as if checking to make sure she was still intact. "They just ate and ate."

Her lower lip began to quiver. I wondered if I should try and hold her. I was about to reach out for her, but she said, "Marty, it was so real."

"You're safe now," I said.

"No, no one's safe. They're out there. We've both seen them."

"They don't know we're here."

She picked up her glass of water and took a slow sip. When she was done, she held the glass with both hands. "I don't know how long that's going to last."

# 21
# A Trek for Food

It's been two days since I last posted. To be honest, I forgot about you. See, there's something about Selena that you need to understand: Time dissolves when she's around. The passing of moments are barely acknowledged, and if they are kept track of, it's done on a subconscious level and never on purpose. You know when to eat, to sleep and all the rest, but I don't recall looking at my watch until just this morning, the digital date informing me how long it's been since I told you about Selena's dream. Some reading this might say two days isn't a long time. You don't understand. In the world I live in, one filled to the brim with the undead, two days is a *very* long time. Add being reunited with the love of your life after you thought you killed her and time has no meaning.

Hold on a second . . .

. . .

. . .

Selena asked what I was doing. I thought it might be best to keep this blog a secret. For now. See, girls are finicky like that: they want a guy who *needs* them, but not one who *really needs* them. The sad part is, it's hard for us guys to find that balance.

Anyway, I just said I was writing down some thoughts about the zombies and coming up with a game plan to keep us safe. In a way, it was partially true, but it's killing me to keep this blog from her. But this thing needs to be written in case something happens to me. There needs to be a record of trying to live on this zombie-infested planet. And if I'm going to be the one to write it, I'm going to do it my way and include the girl of my dreams.

Back to the task at hand: Selena. I know some of you are sick of hearing about her, but it's important I share everything with you. You'll understand in the end—if I live long enough to get to the end or even if there is an end.

Food is scarce. We're not starving, but it's becoming a challenge to find what we need as either what is found is already rotten, or I end up being the one to clean out an abandoned pantry or kitchen cupboard and there's not much there to begin with.

Selena and I went on a food hunt yesterday. She insisted on coming, though I pleaded with her to stay at the apartment for her own safety.

"I'd feel safer if I was with someone," she said. "Besides, I can hold my own, if I need to."

"I'm sure you can," I said, though I didn't really think so. She never struck me as the warrior type. Further—and, yeah, think of me as a politically-incorrect/insensitive/ignorant fool—but, despite the whole "all for equality" mantra that was so prevalent in society, the reality is the children were the first to be eaten, then the women, then the men. Girls are just not as strong as guys. Save for a few exceptions, we dominate. Hunters and gatherers and all that jazz. As for Selena, she's the kind of girl who, when you hug her, you can feel her frailness. Not that she's weak, but her frame is small, and I've never seen her lift anything heavy. Even when she used to give me a good squeeze, there wasn't a moment where I went, "Okay, that's enough."

Digression over.

Selena and I hit the streets. I was armed with my

razor-covered baseball bat. She had a cleaver from the kitchen. Unless we had to weave around fallen vehicles or rubble, I made sure she was beside me the whole time.

It took an hour, but we made a direct line from my apartment north to Chinatown. Back in the day, it was one of the most colourful areas in Comptropolis. The curved and rounded roofs with their swooping eaves stood high and proud over elegant shops, some made of solid glass except for their structural supports. Neon signs hung in windows; others named the restaurant or store in big, bold far-eastern-styled letters. A tourist attraction, sure, but there was more to it than that. There was a sense of history and cultural pride, something that was lost in most other parts of the city when Comptropolis made its mad dash for modernism.

The downside of searching Chinatown for food was the Chinese used a lot of fresh ingredients in their cuisine. By now, all of it would be rotten. However, the Chinese were also wizards at drying foods and I hoped we could round up a bag or two of rice, noodles, powdered soups and dehydrated vegetables.

At the edge of Chinatown, Selena and I stood side by side.

It had been a quiet walk over. Any undead we saw were quickly avoided by us ducking in behind zipcars or under benches or in bus stops. But here in Chinatown, we had a big problem: the undead roamed the streets. Many of them gathered in packs. I counted at least thirty zombies from where I stood.

"Think they see us?" Selena asked. Her voice wavered, and I guessed she was still upset over her dream and what she saw before her was too much. But to be honest, it *is* too much. For anybody.

"Not yet, but they will. All it takes is one. After that,

they *all* see you, like their brains are connected somehow."

"What do we do?"

"Sneak around. I want to hit The Wok over there." I nodded in the restaurant's direction.

Selena peered down the street. It took her a moment, but it appeared she finally saw the burned-out sign reading THE WOK. She took a deep breath and let it out slowly. "What's the plan?"

It was then I really wished she wasn't with me. If anything happened to her . . . (and yeah, I realize my feelings for her are messed up, and I've done things too horrible to be forgiven, but *you* trying living in a world filled with zombies and do better. No, really, go for it. I'll be right here if you need me).

"Here's the deal," I said. "Stay close. They come near, first try to avoid them. If you can't, lay into them with that knife of yours. Just be careful it doesn't get stuck in them and you lose it. Cool?"

"Okay. You be careful."

"I will."

We started in, cautiously, nearly tiptoeing. Less than five feet from where we started and an undead guy with mottled deep gray skin apparently saw us because he changed direction and started toward us, feet dragging. He brushed past another zombie—a girl with no nose and blood running from her chin—his shoulder scraping so strongly against hers it was enough to turn her so she faced us. On our right, another one seemed to see us.

"Keep going straight," I said. "Don't go out of your way to get them." I did want to take my bat across their undead skulls, but with Selena by my side, getting to The Wok in one piece was more important.

We went around another vehicle, eyes trained forward

on the restaurant. More undead turned our way. More drew closer.

The moment the dead guy with deep gray skin brushed his fingers against my shoulder, I swung the bat into his head. The razors caught on his skin and peeled his nose and cheek from his face. I raised the bat high then brought it down on his head. The bone cracked and the creature fell to its knees. Selena yelped. I took the bat across the zombie's head again. Its neck broke and its head snapped to the side; the razors on my bat took more flesh and bone with it. The zombie fell over.

Selena screamed and an undead dude, thick and bloated, had his hand on her shoulder. Shrieking, she tried to pull away. The zombie gripped her right shoulder and jerked her toward him. About to come in with the bat, another zombie stepped in front of me. I jabbed the bat into its chest then brought it around and clocked the creature in the back of the head.

Selena turned on her heels, raised the cleaver, and brought it down on the zombie's wrist. She wasn't strong enough to have sliced clean through, but the force was enough that the undead man paused and looked at his hand. That was enough time for me to make two giant strides over to it and thrust the bat across its skull. The creature fell to the ground. I went over to its arm, put my foot down on it, then ripped the cleaver from its wrist and handed it to Selena.

"Here," I said.

She took it.

"Hold it harder. Try chopping instead of just slamming it into something."

She nodded.

More zombies closed in.

"Watch out," I said, referring to myself, not them.

I lunged forward, bringing my bat down into every undead head that filled my vision. Men, women, even children received a blow to the head. Some stayed down, others didn't. Those who stumbled to the side or fell but got back up received another swing. One guy's head burst on impact. I don't know what that was about. It was almost like hitting a watermelon. Over-decayed, maybe, though his skin wasn't in too bad of shape.

A little girl with no lips grabbed hold of my leg and tried to bite my thigh. I brought the base of the bat in between her face and my leg, then pried it back over my leg like a crowbar, loosening her hold on me. Taking a step away, I wound up and hammered the bat into her face in a golf swing. The force was enough to lift her off her feet and go flying, a spray of blood hitting the air with her.

To my right, Selena hacked into an old man with no shirt. She ripped the cleaver from the side of his neck. Blood spurted out in an arc. She took the knife in on the other side.

"I got it," I said, moving in. She removed the blade, and I took the bat across the old guy's head. The flesh and bones of his neck gave way, and his head went flying off his shoulders.

Taking Selena by the hand, I brought her close then ran with her past a couple zombies and in between two more. We were almost at the restaurant.

"Get behind me," I said and began swinging the bat side-to-side. Every zombie that got close got struck. On one of them, my bat got stuck in between its neck and shoulder and I had to pry it loose while waving off the undead man's hands as he tried to grab me.

With a shriek, Selena brought the cleaver down and into the man's forehead.

"Nice," I said.

"Thanks." She grinned. It was the first time I saw her smile all day.

Forcing myself to remain focused, I took out another zombie, and Selena and I made it to The Wok's front doors. They were glass and the glass was smashed. Others had been here first.

We ran inside and were immediately greeted by a mound of bodies, mostly piles of bones and gobs of dry and wet flesh. Anything obviously humanoid was lost in the gruesome pile.

"Disgusting," Selena said. "Stinks."

"Awful, I know. Let's go."

The groans of the dead filled the air behind us, as did their banging and clamouring as they made their way into the building.

"We don't have much time," I said.

We ran through the dining room, past turned-over tables and strewn-about white tablecloths smeared with blood. I accidentally kicked a severed arm when I ran by it.

We burst through the kitchen doors. Silver pots and pans lay everywhere. Metallic cupboard doors hung open and bare. The deep freeze door at the back of the room was also open.

"Pantry. Pantry. Pantry," I said.

Selena stayed close to me as I walked around and scanned the room.

"Sure this place has food?" she asked.

"I didn't say I was sure. Just never been here. Most everything between my place and Chinatown has been picked clean. This area was the next stop on my list."

Footfalls thumped against the ground in the other room.

"Hurry, Marty. Hurry," she said.
"I know."
But I couldn't see the pantry.
The kitchen door swung open.
The dead shambled in.

# 22
# Just Keep Moving

Selena and I dropped behind a counter loaded with scattered spoons and pots. Both of us breathed quick and short, our breaths echoing the fast beat of our hearts. We looked at each other with wide eyes, knowing the slightest sound would alert the dead to our location. Selena's lower lip began to tremble. I don't know why it happened then, of all times, but tears dripped from the corners of my eyes—not because of fear, but of seeing her so scared. I wished so badly I could just wrap my arms around her and shelter her from the undead lumbering into the kitchen, their groans echoing off the walls.

But I couldn't.

To sit there, eyes closed, pretending we were somewhere else would only ensure our deaths.

So we sat there as still as statues, hoping the undead wouldn't shamble around the whole kitchen. If only they'd just leave. The moments ticked by, time seeming to be caught in a slow drip of molasses.

Selena squeezed her eyes shut when a zombie let out a raspy howl. She broke down, sobbing. She did her best to stifle each choking gasp, but the best she could do was make it sound like some kind of inverted sneeze.

The zombies' footsteps drew closer.

"We're going to have to run," I whispered.

She opened her eyes and nodded, her expression clearly displaying she knew it was her fault the undead heard us, her gaze asking me for forgiveness. Even if we were going to die, of course I'd forgive her.

The dead drew nearer, and I guessed they were right up against the other side of the counter. How many were there, I didn't know.

"Arms up and plow through," I told her. "Let me go first."

I duck-walked past her then drew my arms up so my forearms were held in front of me like a couple battering rams, my bat held vertical like some kind of flag of land and country. Selena held her cleaver aloft.

"Now," I said, and stood quickly. Ignoring the head rush, I rounded the counter and propelled myself forward through a pack of zombies about four bodies thick.

"Run!" Selena screamed from behind.

We headed for the kitchen door, leaving the shamblers behind us. We emerged back into the dining room proper, which was now swarming with the undead. Bat in hand, I went to work bringing its razor-covered end into every rotting head I saw. Blood and skin tore from decaying skulls, sailing through the air like a black, red, and gray mist. Selena grunted behind me as she took the cleaver to anything that came near her. Bodies dropped, and I learned a secret to fighting the undead at The Wok: keep moving. You cannot let yourself become stationary when under attack. Just move, move, move and cut your way through like a madman.

My bat sliced open the chest of a woman, the interior of her breasts sliding out like moldy chicken from a couple wet paper bags. I brought the bat up into the stomach of a dead old man, removing his guts, making them drop out to the floor.

"Get to the door!" I said.

"Should have seen if there was a back one," Selena replied as she drove the cleaver home into a dead teenager's skull.

"Didn't see one running off the kitchen." I took a deep breath, brought my bat against the head of another zombie, then called to her, "We get outside, go right. I think there was an opening there."

"Opening?"

"Not as many zombies."

"Okay."

With a shriek, I ran for the doors, swinging my bat side-to-side, its bladed end tearing into some of the undead, other times serving more as a battering ram, helping to clear the way. Selena was right behind me. The blade of her cleaver nicked the back of my arm. I barely felt it; just a mild sting. I don't think she realized it because she didn't say anything.

We emerged through the broken front doors of The Wok, the zombies out front ambling about in different directions, the majority, however, stumbling toward the restaurant.

"Move!" I shouted.

We headed to the right as planned, taking out as many of the undead as we could. We only fought those who were too close for comfort. When fighting zombies, you see, you don't make active work of it. The goal is to get away and do what needs doing in that regard. Try to take them on like some kind of He-Man and you're dead meat.

Half-eaten bodies lined the streets, all missing their heads. Whether that was from other folks killing the undead or from the undead themselves going after the brains, I'm not sure. Some of the bodies were missing arms and legs. Some just a hand or foot. Guts and blood coated the pavement as if a truck filled with paint cans had crashed and spilled black and red and brown and gray everywhere.

The stench of rot was so thick I think I heard Selena

throw up *while* running behind me. I was about to ask her if she was okay when a dead Asian dude stepped in front of me, hands outstretched. I brought the bat down on his arms, tearing through the rotting skin. The bones within broke and what was left of his arms just dangled there at the elbows. I took the bat to his face and dropped him. Selena and I jumped over the body and kept going.

Finally, we were able to turn a corner into an alley. Fortunately, it was open-ended so if worse came to worse, we wouldn't be trapped.

We stopped and put our hands on our knees.

Selena *did* have a bit of throw up on her mouth. She must have seen me wince because she quickly brought a hand to her face and wiped it away.

"Sorry," she said.

"It's okay. Are you all right?"

"No."

"You hurt?"

"No. Just . . . shaky, grossed out. Sick."

"I know the feeling."

We kept an eye on the mouth of the alley as we caught our breaths.

"So thirsty," I said. "Feels like I'm swallowing a washcloth."

She nodded. "Yup."

A shudder ran through me; my legs were weak. I didn't want to admit it in case Selena was more or less sturdy now. Didn't want to be the weaker one. Not right here.

"Come on," I said, and slowly began backing out of the alley the opposite way we came.

"We're going home, right?" she asked.

Never thought I'd hear her refer to my place as home. "I don't know. We still need food. I'd rather just get it all in one go instead of coming out later."

She didn't reply, and I didn't want to press the issue in case we'd fight or something.

At the mouth of the alley, opening up onto a new street, I stopped, turned around and surveyed the area to get a handle on things.

I didn't like what I saw.

# 23
# Wrong Way

The dead were everywhere. An entire street just loaded with the suckers. The sidewalks, the roads, even some in the building windows.

I've seen zombies before, so their presence wasn't what caught me off guard.

It was their *silence*.

I hadn't heard them when Selena and I were coming up that alley. I hadn't even heard them when I was at the alley's edge.

Something was wrong.

"Marty . . . ?" Selena started.

My heart raced. She gripped my arm, head against my shoulder, trembling.

"We have no choice but to go back the way we came," I said.

"But they're back there, too," she said.

"I know, but there are too many here. There's no way we can—" I cut myself off the moment one of them began to move. Then, like a line of dominoes, they all began to move, heading right for us.

Selena and I tore off back down the alley.

"Hope you have a plan," she said.

*Not really.* "Just keep running. It's call we can do."

When we got back to the street we just came from, I brought my bat up, ready to swing it into any undead skull I saw.

A gray-skinned businessman came up on my right. I took the bat across his head, the blades dragging across his skin, digging deep into the flesh beneath, ripping it from the bone. I pulled the bat back and let him have it again, this time its end cracking the guy's skull and sending him to the ground.

Selena already had her cleaver wedged into an undead teen girl's face. She had to pull it out by putting a palm to the girl's cheek while tugging back on the cleaver.

"Move it!" I said and headed away from the Chinese restaurant and down the street.

"Coming!" she said.

I heard her footfalls behind me.

An old man zombie reached for me. I knocked his arms away with the bat. Selena's footfalls stopped so I looked over my shoulder. She was leaning over an undead kid on the ground, chopping the cleaver into it like a slab of raw steak. Blood and meat sprayed up after each blow.

"That's enough," I said. The old man moved beside me. I laid into him and broke his head open.

She let the kid have it one more time then ran up to me. "Got carried away."

Her hand holding the giant knife shook and her lips trembled. We had to find some place safe and take a break.

I took her by the other hand and we ran a little further down the street, dodging the undead, then rounded into an alley on our right. There was only one zombie in it, which I quickly dispatched with my bat.

"I don't want to stay out here anymore," she said.

"We'll be okay. Just stick together, work together. That's what we were good at, remember?"

She glanced up at me with hopeful eyes, her gaze conveying that, yes, she did remember how much of a good team we really were back in our day.

"You were always there for me," she said.

"I always will be." The words were out before I had time to think about them. In my heart of hearts, yes, I would always be there for Selena. She was my girl, my angel. Ever since I met her, my life in some way was always about her.

Zombies rounded the corner into the alley after us. Selena and I made a break for it and headed toward its opposite end. When we emerged on the street beyond, I checked things out. Over here, the dead's number was thinner. There were still a lot of them—at least ten or so—but they were scattered far enough apart that we wouldn't get cornered.

Fallen zipcars dotted the street, a few in heaps from the day they came crashing down from the sky. Building windows were smashed. Patches of blood stained the concrete.

Some twenty meters to our left was a staircase leading to the old subway system. At the time of the zombie uprising, Comptropolis was in the middle of switching its public transportation to the skytrain, which didn't require underground tunnels and tracks, but instead hovered some fifty meters above street level, weaving its way in between buildings, folks able to get off the skytrain at stops built into the buildings themselves.

"I have an idea," I said and took her by the hand toward the subway entrance.

We ran toward it, weaving around the zipcars. I caught Selena looking in a zipcar's window at the headless corpse of its passenger.

"No time," I said.

She shook her head. "So sad."

"Selena!"

She ran up to me and we headed toward the subway entrance. We managed to avoid the undead shambling toward us and went down the stairs leading to the subway entrance as fast as we could.

"Keep an eye out," I told her.

She got behind me, cleaver ready. "Maybe they'll just fall down the stairs and make it easier for us?"

I couldn't help but chuckle. Man, did I love this girl. "One can only hope."

The subway entrance was a big metal door, locked. One either side of it were glass panes, both miraculously intact.

In my genius, I thought I could whack out the bottom of one of the panes, you know, just have the bottom part break, the rest of it either remaining perfect or just simply spider-webbed but still in place. No go. The entire glass pane shattered when I hit the lower part of it with the bat.

"You realize they'll follow us in," Selena said.

"No choice. They're not here yet, anyway. Maybe we'll be okay. You never know."

She simply rolled her eyes and went in through the glass pane.

Undead moans sounded above.

I followed her.

# 24
# Light in Real Life (Guys are Idiots)

The old underground subway tunnel was dark for the most part, but not so pitch black we couldn't see anything. Far up ahead light streamed in from street level thanks to a large hole in the tunnel's ceiling.

Selena and I walked side-by-side, me with my razorblade-bat at the ready, her with her cleaver. I really hoped we didn't run into any undead down here.

We jumped from the subway platform down onto the tunnel floor. The tracks were clear from what I could see so I suggested we make our way down toward the light and take it from there.

"Sounds fine," Selena said.

I went up to the subway tracks. "Wonder if the power's still on . . ." I spat on them. The gob of spit didn't fizzle. "Nothing. Maybe it's grounded. I don't know."

"Guess the power's up in a few places and that's all," she said.

"Yeah. Ready?"

"Ready."

We walked.

We were silent for the first few minutes; I was so on-edge because of the ordeal above ground that all I could think about was the possibility of having to swing my bat into another zombie's head. Selena seemed to be in the same boat as I. She kept looking around and behind herself, jumping at the slightest sound.

"If they indeed are only after food, they're probably not down here," I told her.

"And you know this how?"

"Because the undead have been around for a while. Anybody they could have eaten down here was probably eaten a long time ago."

My little snippet of information didn't seem to help because she still seemed as paranoid as ever.

Selena coughed and covered her mouth with the back of the hand holding the cleaver.

My heart raced, but down here, it wasn't because of the undead. Those specific palpitations stopped about five or six minutes after we headed toward the light.

Ha. The "light at the end of the tunnel." If only I could transfer that statement to real life.

Being with Selena reminded me of old times when we used to go for long walks, holding each other's hand, sometimes barely speaking for over an hour straight, each other's presence being enough to sustain the mood. Even walking with her in the subway tunnel made my hand ache to reach out and hold her fingers with mine. I wondered what would happen if I tried?

Guys . . . well, we're all just a bunch of big idiots, aren't we? I mean, here I was in the middle of a fantasy: alone with the girl I adored who had broken up with me and wrecked my life long before. You know the saying, "I wouldn't date you even if you were the last man on Earth!" And here I was, possibly the last man on Earth, and if not on the planet, then in the city. And if not in the city, then most likely the last man standing that Selena knew from her life before the zombies rose and took over.

In a stupid and weird way, I was her only option. In

an even weirder—possibly creepy—way, it made me happy.

Selena coughed again. "Excuse me."

"No worries."

At the end of it, though, I'd gone out of bounds. Here we were trying to get away from the undead and all I could think about was the poor girl being cornered because I was the only dude she knew left.

Yeah, guys are idiots.

"What?" she said.

"Huh?"

"You kind of huffed and shook your head."

"Oh, nothing. Just zoned out a bit." *If you only knew what was going through my mind, Selena, you'd probably hate me forever, leave me here and take your chances with the undead. Man, I'm a loser.*

The beam of light streaming into the tunnel grew brighter and wider the closer we got to it. From where we were, I could make out the jagged edges of a rubble heap.

A low moan came from somewhere down the tunnel. Which direction, it was hard to tell. We both froze in our tracks.

"Get ready," I said and tightened my grip on my bat.

We stood there, scanning the tunnel.

There was no second moan or any other sound we could make out. We walked on.

Selena coughed again, this time needing to stop and put her head between her legs to catch her breath when she was done.

"You all right?" I asked, putting my hand on her shoulder.

She swallowed then said, "Yeah. Just got this itch deep down I can't seem to cough up."

"Hate those."

She cleared her throat, spat, then stood. After a deep breath, she was able to continue walking.

After a while we finally made it to the beam of light. Scraps of concrete and metal lay in a giant heap, almost up to the surface. Leading down to it from street level was a portion of the road itself, all broken and suspended downward at an angle, the rebar within stopping it from falling. Shards of glass littered the ground as did burnt seats and scorched metal.

"Weird," Selena said.

"Looks like an explosion," I said. "One of the subway cars?"

"Well, whatever caused it was enough to blow the roof out."

"Yeah, but these things are electric. I'm no engineer, but I don't think gas is a part of the equation."

"Old school technology . . ."

"Foul play. Could be. The riots Comptropolis saw after the undead, the bombs, the madness. We're lucky there's even survivors for the zombies to eat."

She shot me a hard look.

"I mean, it's amazing people even survived."

I put my hands on my hips and surveyed the disarray. There was a gap of at least four feet between the rubble heap and the slanted slab of concrete leading up to the street. The angle seemed climbable even though I figured it was a little more than forty-five degrees.

"We've got to try this," I said.

"What?"

"Climbing out. We got away from the undead. That was our goal."

Selena coughed again, covered her mouth. With a nod she said, "Yeah. I don't want to stay down here any longer than I have to."

"Me neither."

Moans rose on the air from inside the tunnel. These ones were close.

"Together," I said. I held out my hand.

Selena took it.

# 25
# Love

Love is a funny thing.

I know I'm not the first guy to say that. I think Peter Fox said the same thing in his book, *April.* But it's the truth. Love brings out the best in people, but it also brings out the worst. I mean, look at me: if you've been following this journal from the beginning, you've seen what it's made me. I told you about the good times, the bad, and the craziness afterward, namely that of me and my own life and the stupid headspace I found myself in.

Love was one of those things that, growing up, you always thought you'd find. Everyone grows up thinking they'll meet the person of their dreams, get married, get a house, have a couple kids, a dog, maybe even a skyvan. Love is picturesque when you first hear about it. Then it becomes magical—something that, in later years, may even be unattainable but magical nonetheless. And then if you're blessed enough to find it, it *is* magical, and your whole world changes.

Of all things to be thinking of when Selena and I climbed that rubble heap, that's what I thought of.

Love, you see, is no one's master. This is why—after spending time immersed in it—it makes you lose control, whether for good or bad. It's why you'll move heaven and earth to make your girl happy. It's why you think of killing yourself when she breaks your heart. It's why it stays with you until the next time you see her, and why it stays with you when you know you'll never see her again.

Time . . . also belongs to love. Even on the rubble

heap, time was meaningless, and I could think and feel and dream and reminisce, and what might have been a couple of minutes in the real world, was time enough for me to think of all these things I'm writing down now.

Love gives life and love kills. And, as of this writing, I've tasted both and even *lived* in both. It's making me ramble right now because if this journal is indeed all that's left of me, and I do get eaten by the undead, I want a full record of what it was like to live in this time of zombies, and what it was like bouncing from a broken heart to feeling like life was worth living again . . . even in a zombie-infested world.

On that rubble heap, Selena coughed behind me as I led her up. She slipped on a patch of gravel and had to yank her hand free from mine so she could stop herself from landing face first against the debris.

"Are you all right?" I asked and held out my hand again. Losing the touch of her fingers made me feel like *I* was the one falling and not the other way around.

She steadied herself on all fours and couldn't stop coughing.

"What is it?" I asked. "The dust?" It wasn't all that dusty but perhaps she was more sensitive to it than I.

All she could do was shake her head; she was still coughing.

I crouched down next her to as best as I could, careful to have my feet firmly planted so I didn't do a nosedive off the rubble heap and back into the subway tunnel below.

"Selena . . ." I said.

Finally, she took a big gasp of air then cleared her throat. "I'm o—I'm okay."

"You sure?"

She merely nodded again.

"Okay, then let's get going." I helped her up, swayed backward a little, then righted myself so I could get her firmly on her feet once more.

We slowly made our way up to the much-smoother cement slab that led up to street level. I was careful not to get too far ahead of her this time.

Too far ahead.

In some ways, I think it was my jumping the gun that landed us in trouble back in the old days. Sometimes, what happened before is as clear as crystal. Other times, I could barely remember what went on.

Love does that to you: makes you see and feel what you need in the moment you're in and blinds you to what really is.

I think it was my "getting ahead" of her that scared her off after we broke up. She knew I still loved her with all my heart, even obsessively so. I couldn't wrap my head around how that could frighten her. If anything, I figured having someone love you *too* much was a good thing, especially in a world filled with so many cold hearts. Some of you now might think I've gone too far on this, talk about how much I loved Selena too much. Guess it just proves my point. Maybe you never fell for someone so hard they became your whole world, and you were nothing without them.

In the end, Selena probably knew I didn't let her go. There were times, believe me, when I tried. In fact, I tried *everything*. Books, music, self-help videos, talking it out with friends—all of it for naught.

Coming out into the light and getting our feet on a less slippery surface made the rest of our climb much easier. Selena stopped once to catch her breath, which I figured had been tied to her coughing. I felt more or less fine.

We got to the top and immediately surveyed the street. So far, the undead were nowhere to be seen, but I knew better than to just stand there and wait to see if they'd show up.

"Marty . . ." Selena said.

I glanced over to her, and she was in the midst of lifting her hand to my shoulder.

Then she collapsed.

# 26
# I Left my Life

"No!" I went close to her, dropped my bat and got down beside her. "Selena, wake up. Come on, you have to wake up." I leaned over and listened for breathing. I had my ear nearly right against her lips. All that came out was a soft wheeze. I put my head to her chest. Her heart was still beating, but the beats were very far apart.

"Pleasepleasepleasepleaseplease . . ." I said and gently cupped my hands around her head and lifted it slightly off the ground. "Wake up, Selena. We can't stay here." Tears licked the corners of my eyes. I couldn't lose her. Not again.

Moans drifted on the air and an immediate shudder went through me. I checked back over my shoulder. A string of undead had rounded a corner not far from us and were stumbling down the road in our direction.

"Selena, get up! They're coming!"

She lay there, still, almost peaceful. I listened for breath again. The groans of the dead must have obstructed my hearing because I couldn't hear anything escaping her lips. I checked her chest once more. Her heart beat so slowly, barely there.

The zombies drew nearer. There were six of them.

"Come on," I said and scooped my arms up under her. I adjusted my grip around her small frame and got to my feet. She was light, maybe around a hundred and twenty pounds. I took a few steps further from the dead, then quickly rounded back.

My bat.

The undead were maybe forty feet away. They'd be here any moment.

Selena still in my arms, I crouched down and with my right hand felt around between the back of her knees and the ground, searching for the bat's handle. I found it and got my fingers around it—backwards, so my thumb and forefinger were at the bottom of the handle—then pushed my heels against the ground and stood. The bat dangled beneath Selena's legs. I checked her face. Her head and neck were limp. She was completely unconscious.

As fast as I could, I started jogging down the road, already thinking three or four blocks ahead, the goal being to get back to my place as soon as possible if I couldn't find another hideaway spot on the way there.

More zombies came out from the alleys and from around corners. The nearest group of them, all decayed, their stink reaching my nostrils, were a mere twenty feet behind me.

Heart racing, blinking the tears from my eyes, I moved as quickly as I could. I went down the road, hopped over a curb, and rounded a black skyvan that had marooned itself there in days long gone.

"Wake up, Selena!" I screamed. I didn't mean to, but the words just bursted out without restraint. I needed her awake.

I needed her *alive*.

The next corner was a messy intersection of an upside-down waste truck, a few zipcars, and bunch of debris and litter. The ground was cracked in a wild spider web all around the vehicles. These no doubt fell from the sky when the world changed and everything started dying.

The street was blocked so I jogged as fast as I could to the next corner.

The undead moaned behind me.

I checked over my shoulder. More must have joined their kin because a rotted hand with one finger missing went to grab me. I pushed my jog into overdrive and the creature missed.

I rounded another fallen vehicle, then my foot caught something hard and slick and my right heel went out from under me as if I was on ice. I fell on top of Selena, her limp form rolling with the impact. My knee scraped the ground under her. My elbows were scraped up to heck as well.

The moans of the dead loud and raspy, I worked quickly to get my arms back under Selena, but before I could, I was grabbed from behind and a rotted face came down on my shoulder. I thrashed about, elbowed the creature in the face, and got to my feet.

There were four of them at first, two old ladies with open stomachs, their guts hanging out, and two young men, one with an eye missing, the other just a mess of torn-up flesh and flaky gray skin.

The two young men knelt down beside Selena and pawed at her body.

"Get off her!" I yelled and ran over to them. I kicked one in the head, knocking him back. I spun around to do the same to the other, but one of the old ladies grabbed my wrist and jerked me in her direction. I kicked her in the shins, her rotting bones snapping from the blow. She fell down and I jumped a couple steps back.

My bat. It was beside Selena. I went to grab it, but more undead crowded about the two young guys clawing at my girl.

"No!" I screamed. My eyes immediately clouded over with tears. I wiped them away and started to push through the undead. Many shoved me back, as if Selena was more important to them than me, another *live* human being trying to rescue a loved one.

When I was able to poke my head between them, my heart cried out within me. Their fingers dug into Selena's flesh, blood gushing from the holes they tore. They ripped at the meat beneath her skin and brought it to their foul lips.

I wanted to scream, to curse them, to cry out to God for help—but my voice caught and all I managed was a weak rasp.

A big undead black guy shoved his hand against my stomach, his fingers opening and closing as if trying to dig into my flesh. For a moment, I considered letting him, but then—at that time, as if a new idea and something never thought of before—I realized I could run.

I could get away from there and survive.

But Selena . . .

The undead's lips smacked; their moans escalated. More zombies joined the horde.

I ran. I didn't want to, but I ran.

Adrenaline surged through me and I gave it everything I had.

I left Selena.

I left my love.

I left my life.

# 27
# Tremors

A few blocks away, the tremors started. At first, I thought it was the monstrous horde of undead causing it, their decayed and rotted feet smacking against the pavement so hard it caused the ground to shake.

But it wasn't them.

It was me.

Every bone in my body shook as if I had my finger in an electrical socket. The next thing I knew, my legs gave out from under me and I fell to the sidewalk alongside the old theatre, the kind that played holographs once the flicks left the "real" theatres with the bigger auditoriums. I remained there on my knees, rocking back and forth, my muscles locking, my heart slamming against the inside of my chest a trillion miles an hour. It would only be just a few more seconds, I thought, until the heart attack kicked in and I'd keel over only to find myself reanimated a few minutes later.

Selena.

She was dead.

And I . . . I left her there. I left her!

For all my bravado and pining over her, for all the endless fantasies where I told her I'd do anything for her, even give up my life—I left her there.

I could barely glance over my shoulder, my muscles were so stiff. The undead were a good ways off, but I could see them shambling down the road toward me.

Let them come. I deserved what they'd do to me. I deserved having my guts ripped out and eaten like spaghetti.

I deserved to die.

It was only a scant few minutes ago I was with Selena. Just a few minutes.

A few minutes ago, she was alive, still here on this earth with me.

A few minutes ago, there was hope for a future together. A small hope, but a hope nonetheless. Now all that was taken away both by my cowardice and those blasted zombies.

Death knew no bounds.

But if I stayed, I'd be dead too. To tell you the truth, I really didn't know what was worse right then. The pain inside was so large, so *alive*, that even the memory of any other emotion could not be recalled.

On that sidewalk, my heart pounding, my body shaking, I tried to get on my feet only to find myself crawling like a baby instead. I could barely move, only able to manage an inch at a time. The undead behind me were moving faster than I was.

I heard their moans on the air. I checked back over my shoulder again. I estimated it'd take them maybe two minutes to reach me if I didn't somehow get away.

For a moment, I thought about what it would be like to have them dig into my flesh, to pull my skin and muscles apart like tissue paper. I imagined the pain, and to be honest, it seemed better than the sharp, deep hollow agony that pierced my heart and made me sick to my stomach.

Three thoughts were very clear, as if each were being projected back at me from a mirror: One was losing the girl I loved again. To see her so helpless, to see her murdered. To never see her again.

The second was the loss of myself all over again

because I knew what it was like to go crazy and see your life in the bizarre before-and-after photo when losing someone you love.

The final thought was the zombies. And though their presence almost seemed peripheral at that moment, it was hard to believe that that moment was actually real and there were real dead people walking toward me that wanted nothing more than to eat me.

I crawled, forcing my limbs to move, my palms scraping against the sidewalk, my feet dragging behind me, my knees grating against the ground.

The zombies moaned.

I cried out, full and loud. Pure sound, raw emotion.

Selena and survival were my only thoughts.

Selena's survival . . . my only thought.

Her death.

My own inevitable to come.

*Let me run. Oh, God, please hear me and let me run.* Could there be redemption? Would there be a miracle?

I crawled faster, grunting and growling as I propelled my body across the pavement.

The stench of the undead grew fuller. I checked again to see how far away they were, but the tears in my eyes made everything a blurry mess so it was too difficult to tell.

"Push yourself," I said. "Come on. Go." I moved as quickly as I could, now moving at a slow walker's pace along the ground.

My muscles still shook, but the painful vibrations surging through my bones had subsided to a dull hum.

"Stand," I said. *If not for yourself, then for her.* "Get up."

I pulled my feet under me and held my hands out for balance as I slowly got myself upright. Head woozy, everything within tingling, I stepped forward. It was like walking on a tight rope and I thought I would go down again. Instead, my steps increased in speed and I was able to move at a brisk walk down the sidewalk. I turned at the corner, hoping I'd lose the dead.

I needed to get home.

The undead calls droned on the air.

My heart ached.

I wiped the tears from my eyes and headed across the street, traveled down another sidewalk length before turning into a back alley. There were no zombies here, and I hoped my little zigzag pattern was enough to elude the undead behind me.

One last thought became clear: Selena was back there . . . what was left of her.

It was all my fault.

# 28
# Release

The more I walked, the easier it became. Like most things, all you needed was a little distance. The alley I stood in was bare: just me, litter, a couple quick-disposers, and the smell of an unattended sewer thickening the air.

It's one thing to say you knew what to do in a survival situation, quite another to actually do it. However, there is one secret—priority. So I channeled the notion inward, setting aside images of Selena being torn apart, our time together, the words exchanged, and simply focused on the task at hand.

I needed to get home. I could let loose there, cry, drink, just go crazy, if I really needed to. But until then, yeah, I just simply needed to get there.

My plan to elude the undead coming after me succeeded and that horde was somewhere else. It didn't matter where as long as they were away from me. I wandered down the alley, ears cocked and fists ready.

At the mouth of the alley, the street running adjacent to it was cluttered like most of the others. All those crashed vehicles, windshields splotched with blood, scraps of dried leftover flesh dotting the pavement. I used to be one for peace and quiet. I used to enjoy sitting in the silence of my place, the silence itself almost audible, but in that oh-so-good soothing way. (You know the kind.) Nowadays, what I wouldn't give for a little noise, the human kind. Chatter, skyvans and zipcars tearing through the sky, people laughing, folks yelling, horns honking, sirens blaring. All I had now were my thoughts and whatever songs I could remember playing through my brain in an effort not to go mad from the quiet.

As much as I wanted to run that oldie but goodie, "Pour Some Sugar on Me," through my mind, I fought it back and decided I'd sit in my living room later and replay then. For now, I needed to focus on my exact location, my exact task.

Weaving my way in between the smashed cars, stepping on glass-littered pavement, I headed across the street, hoping the next alley about a block to the right was just as empty as the one I came out of. When I reached it, my heart sank at the sight of a lone undead, shuffling toward me. His arms hung loose at his sides, one of his hands missing. His feet were turned inward, making his steps all the more awkward. I was surprised he was even able to maintain balance at all. The guy wore a dark gray suit, a bow tie loose against his scrawny neck. The man's skin was so sickly gray that had he been naked, he could almost camouflage directly with the surrounding pavement. Dark red and black scabs dotted his skull, their presence growing thicker around his deeply-sunken eyes. Part of his nose had dried up and rotted off a long time ago.

I made my way toward him; not directly at him, mind you, but in his general direction. At first, I walked the left side of the alley. When the creature finally took notice of me, he started to stumble in my direction. I went to the right. The man stopped, seeming to debate some kind of decision, then began shambling to my side of the alley.

He was only ten feet away when I realized I could feign going to one side then sprint past him along the other.

Instead, I chose to adjust my path to the middle of the alleyway. I checked once over my shoulder to make sure the path was clear behind me. It was. The zombie by now had adjusted himself as well and he and I walked toward each other.

Four feet now.

Already the creature's hand and arms were raised, ready to grab me.

For a microsecond, I wanted him to . . . just so I could be with Selena again. Another microsecond and that thought was gone and I brought my forearms down along his, snapping his arms back down to his sides. Fist cocked, I threw a hook across his jaw, my knuckles connecting with his chin so perfectly his jaw bone snapped and tore through his rotted flesh on the follow through. The crusty-skin-coated jaw bone hit the pavement and almost before I even noticed, I came up with my left fist and hook punched his head from the other side. The force of the blow threw the zombie's head to its left. It raised its arms and, using the same maneuver, I slammed them back down again. This time I brought my foot up and kicked it in the stomach. Its body rocked back a step.

Then I let loose, hammering my fists against its face so hard and quick the thing didn't even have a chance to lock eyes with me again. Once more it tried to raise its arms. I grabbed its right arm and pulled it with all my might. The creature's body jerked forward then a dry rip like a piece of toast being torn cut through the air as I dislodged its arm from its socket and pulled it through the creature's suit sleeve. I swung the arm across the zombie's head like a bat before letting the arm go and going back to work on beating the hell out of the thing.

I punched its face, kicked it in the neck, slapped its chest, then sent it to the ground by kicking its knees out from under it, breaking them in the process. The thing landed on its back and I pounced on it like a bloodthirsty jaguar. Its one remaining arm—the one without the hand—swatted at me from the side while I brought blow after blow down into its skull. Its cheekbones cracked beneath my fists then busted inward. Its dried skin and powdery blood blew up around my fingers.

Not wanting to breathe any of that crud in, I got to my feet and brought my heel down on its face over and over until there was nothing left but a nasty mess of crusty skin and brittle bone. I even brought my heel down on its neck—as if it needed to breathe—and stomped on its neck so much the bone, cartilage and flesh tore clean from its body.

I spat on him, cursed him, and kicked his head down the alley like a soccer ball.

I got back on its torso and hammered away on its ribs, digging and clawing at its chest, tearing away the suit and shirt and delivered punches and slaps to its rotted frame.

Fatigue hitting me like a bear hug from Hell, I only stopped when the thing's rotten innards started flying up around me. I fell over to the side of the body and lay there gazing up at the sky. So blue. Very few clouds.

Normal . . . just . . . normal.

I nearly forgot where I was and what I'd just done.

The calls of the undead broke me from my trance. I sat up, still alone in that alley, the decapitated monster beside me, and took a deep breath. Finally, I stood and made my way home.

# 29
# Recap

In case you're only tuning in now, or something has happened to the webfeed and this broadcast of my journal is only now reaching you thanks to undead interference, I just simply want to start by saying my name is Marty. I'm the sole survivor of the planet Earth. I don't have great power, nor do my abilities exceed that of mortal men. I didn't get here in a rocket ship nor am I fighting for truth, justice, and decency.

These days, I'm just fighting to stay alive, and this journal is helping me do that.

I've recorded everything I could for you as things happened. Sometimes I had to wait before I could sit down in front of my screen and type out my thoughts. To be honest, my thoughts are all a jumble, and I'm hankering for the soothing arms of alcohol to keep the insanity at bay. At the same time, I'm too scared to booze up because there's the chance I could lose myself once inhibitions are shed and might never recover. You might even have noticed my abstaining from alcohol by how—what's the way to say this? "Better-worded"?—these entries have become.

I need to keep my head together, need to stay grounded, especially after what happened.

In case you're just joining me, Comptropolis—and the world over—has been invaded by the undead. We're talking zombies, reanimated and deceased human beings. They kill, and they eat us, and if they don't devour you completely, their bites infect you and transform you into one of them. You still die, but you do come back, moving, hungry, having a thirst for human blood and flesh.

This whole journal started as a way to not only try and document my survival—maybe even a call for help across what's left of the Net—but also as a way to cope with a relationship gone bad and the loss of true love.

You see, I live in a world of death: physical and emotional. Aside from my pulse, some days it feels like I'm no different than the zombies that stalk the city streets.

Selena, my ex-girlfriend and love of my life, surfaced at my apartment recently. She came to me because everyone else she knew was gone, and she knew that if I was still alive, my door would always be open to her. We even spent some time together, but on a food run we came under attack by a horde of zombies. She got sick while we were out and eventually collapsed. I tried to carry her here—home—so I could care for her. Instead, the undead overtook us, and I had no choice but to leave her body to be devoured.

I hate myself for it. I'll never forgive myself for what I did. Not only did I lose her all over again, but I lost what might have been a chance at happiness.

Death came for me, but instead of taking me out directly, it once again had its way by destroying what was left of my heart.

I apologize to those out there reading this and recapping things like I am, but I ask for your indulgence because there might be those out there who don't know what's going on and might be wondering what this partial journal they've stumbled upon is all about. We're all in this together, remember? Strength in numbers and all that.

Are there any numbers, though? The haunting feeling that I'm all alone has been with me since I got home. I was already giving into the notion when I first started writing this, but when Selena showed up, I admit a part of me considered there were others out there too. And if not, then maybe who . . . or whatever finds these bytes of information can catch a glimpse of what it was like to live during these dark times.

I just hope the darkness doesn't last forever. To have a break . . . even a hope . . . the words escape me.

Are you there? Is anyone reading this? Or is this just one giant exercise in catharsis and that's all?


. . .


. . .


My heart's racing. Something knocked on my door. It could be *them*, the undead.


. . .


There it goes again. Something's not right. If it was a zombie or more, they'd just slap at the door with decaying palms, hoping that eventually it'd give up and fall down. I don't have any weapons. I dropped my bat coated with razorblades when trying to fight off the dead earlier.


. . .


I can't take this. The bangs are becoming more urgent now. Hold on. I'm going to check to see what's going on.


. . .


. . .

# 30
# Broken

Things are getting worse and this might be my last entry. I . . . it's like someone took my brain and threw it in a pot, only to boil it a thousand times over then stick it back in my head.

I'm losing it.

This city . . . the undead . . . it's finally taken me down.

You look in a mirror and see yourself staring back. You might like what you see, you might not. But it doesn't matter how you feel about yourself because at the end of it all, it's still *you* looking at you. You *know* you're real, you know your thoughts, your feelings, even the taste in your mouth. You know it's you looking at yourself.

I don't know me anymore. My head is so full and all I get are static images of soggy cardboard instead of my brain. All I get is a honeycomb with a thousand entry points, each hole leaking out what's left of my sanity.

You don't know what I'm talking about, do you?

Just need to tell you how I feel, what's going through my head.

I was just at my door.

I checked the peephole.

I saw Selena.

Even now, as I'm typing this, she's banging on the door, screaming for me to let her in.

Inside myself, all I hear is me screaming that she's dead, that there's no way that's her. Intellectually, I know better. I know that it's either a ghost beyond my door out to slit my throat for letting the real Selena die the way she did, or I've completely lost it.

This is where obsession with a girl leads to the slippery slope of a psychotic break. This is the part where I become the monster, and she is forever cemented as the victim.

This is the part where I become worse than the walking dead outside because I *know* better than to allow my fixation on a relationship-gone-wrong become some sort of an imaginary reality, whereas the dead outside act the way they do because they function on pure instinct.

Selena . . . banging on my door.

If I answer—if I let her in—what does that say about me?

If I could step outside myself and watch me open that door and somehow see what's really going on, would I only see myself opening a door to nothing at all, *react* to nothing at all, even talk to nothing at all?

My apartment door is more than just a door right now. It's a portal into a state of mind that could end up killing me in the end.

Selena, the zombies, the isolation, the heartbreak—it's finally ripping me apart . . . silently, but eventually.

In one way or another, the next few moments will decide my fate.

If I open that door, I will no longer be the man typing this.

I will have become something else.

But—there's always a "but"—if that *is* indeed Selena out there, if somehow she's alive and her body has been put back together, then I can't just leave her there banging on my door. If she needs help and has come to me like she did before . . .

That banging.
My girl.
I have to let her in.

# 31
# Delusions of Selena

Have you ever looked at a dead person?

Death . . . it's one of those things our brains aren't built for. We see the person in front of us yet know there's no one there at the same time. It's the same brain freeze I get when I see the undead walking—ghosts, physical forms with no substance.

It was like that with Selena.

I let her into my apartment, not knowing if it *was* a ghost coming to haunt me or if, somehow, she was healed and back from the dead. Even stranger—back from the dead in a *good* way.

She didn't shamble. Didn't have gray skin. No bruises or cuts or gashes. Just my girl. And she was beautiful even in the filthy garbage bag she wore.

Just like . . . before.

When I opened the door, she ran in, shoved it closed behind herself, then threw her arms around me and held me so tight I couldn't breathe.

"You're alive," she said.

I couldn't find the right words to respond. The best I could come up with was a gentle, "So are you."

I didn't know if I was holding a ghost right then or someone with special healing abilities . . . and I didn't care. Not when it came to her. When you lose something, you'd give anything to get it back, risk it all and just be happy you got a second chance no matter how it came.

"You're shaking," she said as she pulled away. "Did they get you? You know, those people outside?"

I simply shook my head.

"Good. There was no one else to turn to and I knew . . . I knew you'd help me if you were still . . ." She didn't finish but I knew what she meant.

Then I processed what she said. "Wait. You knew I'd help you if . . . um, if what?"

"If you were still alive."

"What do you mean?"

"What do you mean what do I mean? Still alive. Breathing. Living. Not one of those creatures."

I furrowed my brow. Was she okay? Didn't she know? "Selena, the undead have been around for a while. Don't you know that?"

She appeared as if to say something then held back. Her eyes searched the air, as if seeing something I couldn't. "I came here. I saw those things."

"Where were you? How did you—?"

"I was home."

Déjà vu hit me like a punch to the face. We had a conversation like this before. She had on the garbage bag, but this time she wasn't hurt.

"Selena, we've already crossed this road. Don't you remember? This isn't normal. We were just together. We were . . . and then . . ." Why couldn't I tell her what happened? It was those eyes. Her beautiful brown eyes. The way she held my gaze told me everything. She *didn't* remember. She looked at me with nothing but question marks for irises, her brow slightly furrowed as if *I* was the one with the screwed-up memory. And to be honest, that very well could be.

The blessed relief at her resurrection fled and I wondered if I was truly talking to someone or, in reality, was merely talking to myself. This shouldn't be so hard.

Are you supposed to entertain imaginary friends? Or

do you give in to the delusion because if you don't your brain—that created the delusion in the first place—*needs* to take part in the fantasy or it'll fry itself from within?

All I could say was, "Are you real?"

Her gaze softened and she smiled just a little in that way where you knew she was happy and thought you were cute. "I'm real, Marty."

I took her in my arms again. She didn't embrace me back right away, but after a moment, she held me tight.

Ghost or not, we were together.

# 32
# On the Move Part One

I'm writing this on a telecom handheld, one I swiped from a corpse after I drove my razor-bat into its head. Please excuse any typos or lowercase words. My hands are shaking.

The telecom seems to have a signal. At least the display says it does. Whether this is joining up with the regular entries I've posted, I don't know. I'm doing this "just in case."

Selena was like the last one—if I could say such a thing—in that she was worn and tired. She napped on my couch. I paced the room, out of a trance of "at least we were together" and looking at her as objectively as I could, wondering what or who it was I was really looking at. Like before, wondering if the girl in front of me was actually real or some mad hallucination. Regardless, I watched her, reminisced a little bit, then grew so uneasy with her presence that bile snuck up the back of my throat and spilled over into my mouth. I left the room to go spit in the kitchen sink. Right in the middle of doing so, Selena screamed. Glass broke. I spat out the wad in my mouth then ran back into my living room only to find Selena had smashed the front window and was up against the frame, my lamp in her hand.

"What are you doing?" I shouted.

She didn't reply but instead searched the ground below. I went to her side and saw the walking dead gathered outside my building, six of them.

I pulled her away from the window. "They'll see you."

She elbowed me in the gut, ran up against the window frame again, and this time threw the lamp out the window. I heard it crash somewhere on the other side, down below.

"Are you crazy?" I asked.

She shoved me aside again with both palms to my chest, searched the room, then grabbed my clock. She hurled it out the window, too.

"Leave me alone!" she shrieked at the living corpses below.

"Selena!"

She ran past me, went into the kitchen and ripped the pots and pans from the cupboard. She tore back into the living room, each hand clutching a pot by the handle.

She swung one at me the moment I came near so I jumped out of the way. She returned to the window and hurled the pots down at the dead.

"Now they know someone is in here for sure," I said. "There will be others. Lots of them."

She ignored me and hurried back to the kitchen for more pots. I ran after her. She stood with a pan and a pot in her hands. I jumped at her and dragged her to the floor.

"Stop it!" I said.

"They have to die!" she said, her eyes wild.

"You're not going to kill them with what you got. Think about it."

She jerked around beneath me. "Get off me!"

"No! Shut up and listen to me. You don't know what you're doing."

"I can't take it anymore."

"Neither can I, but don't you know what you're doing? You're throwing pots out the window, for crying out loud."

"I have to hurt them."

"Not like this."

"Please! Let me kill them!"

"Snap out of it." I reached for her hands and managed to pull the pots away. I tossed them to the side of the kitchen floor; they crashed against the cupboards.

Selena lay there, arms spread out, wailing at the top of her lungs.

A shudder ran through me. She was crazy.

At least right now.

I got to my feet and carefully walked over to the window. I peeked out as best I could, hoping I wasn't seen. The dead stood below, a couple of them looking up, the rest just rocking side-to-side, seeming oblivious to what was going on.

From the kitchen, Selena spoke, her voice thick with tears. "Never again. Never again. Never go on top of me again!"

I didn't know if I should let her cry it out, clean out her system, or if she indeed was having a meltdown and any interference on my part would only make things worse.

The zombies remained below.

I went back to the kitchen, knowing that to leave Selena alone would be a bad idea. When I came back, she was still on the floor, this time with her hands covering her eyes. I sat down beside her, tears of worry forming in my own eyes.

"It's dark," she said. "So dark."

"What's dark?" I asked as gently as I could.

"This world. Me. So many of them."

"I don't . . . I don't know what you mean." What I meant was I got what she was saying, but I didn't know the exact circumstance she was referring to. Then I asked,

"Before, when you were sleeping, was it a dream? Did you dream about . . . them?"

She slowly pulled her hands away from her eyes, her gaze blank. "Yes."

# 33
# On the Move Part Two

Telecom handheld transmission:

We didn't stay in my apartment long. The undead below broke into the building. I don't know how. They're strong, sure, but smart? No, and in order for strength to be effective, you need to have a certain amount of wits about you. Either way, they got in not long after I asked Selena about her dream.

In a panic and knowing going out the front door was a deathtrap, we ran down the hallway and headed for the back door. The undead were there too. They hadn't gotten through the door, but we heard them outside just beyond it.

We were trapped.

The only option was to hole up in the laundry room. It was in the basement, the door heavy, and it had a lock. I should know because when I first went to use the washing machine when I moved in here, I locked myself in, not knowing where the lock release was on the door.

Anyway, we ran that way. Just as we entered the room, I saw the dead at the other end of the hallway, making their way toward us. There was a pack of them, probably around ten.

For a moment, I thought I saw Selena among them, her face bitten off at the cheek, dried blood running down her jaw and neck. Then I glanced forward and was relieved to see she was still with me at the laundry room entrance.

What that little episode was, I don't know.

We got into the room, closed the door, locked it, and a few seconds later endured the dull thumps of dead fists banging the metal-lined door on the other side.

Sitting in the dark, Selena and I huddled next to each other, our hands over our ears, the dull beats of the dead against the door in time with the rapid beat of our hearts.

They wouldn't be getting in. As said, the door was too heavy, and it was locked.

Our problem was how we were going to get out.

"I guess we can wait until they're gone," Selena shouted above the thumping.

I bobbed my head side-to-side. "Maybe. Who knows when that'll be, though."

She merely nodded.

There was no way to tell exactly how many zombies were in the building but judging by the pounding on the door and the sound of heavy footfalls above, each floor would soon be covered in the diseased corpses. I could only imagine them knocking down the doors to each suite, even getting into mine. After I locked it and rummaging through my stuff for something to eat.

My computer. My journal.

As I send you this transmission, I don't know if I'm going back. I hope my previous entries are still intact on my hard drive. If not, I guess I can lift them off the blog itself, if needs be. Regardless, I wasn't ready to leave home.

It was in that dark laundry room with the sounds of the dead echoing throughout it that Selena began to shake. At first, I thought it was merely a shiver, but when she started coughing and fell into a seizure, all I could do was lay her down, hold her head and let her body work it out.

# 34
# On the Move Part Three

Telecom handheld transmission:

It was happening again, me caught in a world of death.

Selena shook and convulsed in my lap, a yellow milky foam dribbling out the corners of her lips.

The zombies banged on the door to the laundry room, the incessant thuds making it difficult to concentrate.

"Selena, please, you have to stop," I said, but why I said it I didn't know. Probably just voicing my thoughts.

She kept shaking, her body bouncing up and down in rollercoaster-like waves.

Heart racing, I asked her if there was anything I could do. She didn't reply, and her eyes were rolled back in their sockets. For a brief moment, I thought she was trying to look up at me, but I had lost her beautiful brown-eyed gaze as the whites of her eyes became all I saw.

The undead beyond the door continued drumming against it.

Selena stopped shaking. Her body kicked out a few more jolts then lay still.

Tears in my eyes, I gently brushed her hair off her face and leaned in, listening for breath. There was none. I put her head on the ground and started CPR. Each press of my palms against her chest grew more and more intense; each time it seemed her non-responsiveness intensified even though I know now it had only been my imagination.

Why was this happening? How many times could I lose her?

I didn't know what was worse right then, losing Selena from my life, but knowing she was alive somewhere, possibly happy, or losing her and watching her die. After all, they both ended with the same result—her absence from me.

Seemed selfish, I know. But unless you've walked this road, you can't say anything. More specifically, unless you've walked this road several times like I have, you have no right to say anything.

At all.

The zombies kept beating their decaying fists against the heavy door.

———

Around an hour later, I was alone in that room. No longer able to look at Selena's deceased form, I carefully laid her down in the janitor's supply closet in the corner of the room and closed its door. It was cruel because she deserved a proper burial, but at the same time, I needed space and given all that I'd been through, I decided to cut myself some slack.

The zombies had stopped beating on the door, but they hadn't left. Their hollow moans still filled the hallway beyond, their deathly groans coming in through the gap between the door and floor.

I lay in a fetal position on the ground, balling my eyes out over my loss.

Over my life.

Over myself.

Yeah, it was a real pity party, but you'd have one too

if you were in my shoes.

I didn't how much time passed, but a dull thump came from the janitor closet. Immediately, I leapt to my feet and cautiously approached it.

Another thump came from behind the door.

No, it couldn't be. Not like this. She was dead. She was—

Not Selena. Please, God, don't let her become one of them.

The thumping grew consistent, and I could imagine her behind the door, stepping up to it, bumping into it, stepping back, then coming at it again. Over and over.

My baby. Not you too.

If I opened the door, I could be dead real soon. If I didn't, then there was a good chance the bumping into the door would grow more aggressive and alert the others in the hallway outside the laundry room there was still something for them to get at.

"Please," I whispered. "Please be okay."

I put my hand on the doorknob and slowly turned it. I took a large step back as I let the door swing all the way open.

Out of the shadows, Selena emerged, her head cocked slightly to one side. Her mouth hung slack; her eyes remained rolled back in their sockets. She stumbled toward me.

"Selena?"

She stopped, turned her head in my direction, then adjusted her footing, this time coming directly at me. A few seconds later, she raised her left hand. I touched her fingers. They were ice cold. Her hand gripped mine and she started to pull herself closer. I yanked my hand away and darted for the far side of the room and scanned it up and down for something to defend myself with. Nothing.

Nothing lethal, anyway.

Selena slowly walked toward me.

I stepped to the side. When my foot came down, it landed on the ground harder than I wanted. Her head immediately craned in the direction of the sound and then she started heading my way.

My girl was gone.

It was a feeling; it was a thought. Its reality sunk in quicker than I expected and I immediately knew I had to get rid of her otherwise I'd be her lunch soon enough.

I let her get close to me before carefully moving out of her way in a semicircle. My goal was to get to the closet she had just come out of. There had to be something in there I could use to defend myself.

Keeping one eye on her, the other on the closet, I inched my way there, each footstep I took as light as I could possibly make it.

Once at the closet, I peered in and scanned the shelves. Nothing but a bunch of cleaning supplies, a mop and bucket, a broom, some boxes and—the broom.

I pulled it out. It wasn't too thick, but thick enough I couldn't break it over my knee.

Slowly, I kept my circular pattern and went to the far corner of the room while Selena was at the other, her head weaving side-to-side as she tried to find me.

I had only one chance at this, and I had to make it quick. I held the broom handle with one hand, leaned it on an angle and put my foot down on its head. Quickly, and as hard as I could, I stomped down halfway between the top of the handle and the broom's head. *Crack!* The wood splintered but didn't break.

Selena turned around and faced me. She raised her arms, her fingers rigid like claws.

I stomped down on the broom again. It snapped this

time, but not cleanly. I had to—

She was close, like six feet away.

I flipped the broom over and came at it from the other side. The wood broke. I let the straw end fall to the floor and I got the handle end ready.

"Please, Selena," I said. "If you can hear me, you need to stop. I don't want to—"

But there was no response in that dead face. No sign she recognized my voice. Not the slightest hint of contemplation.

So be it, I said to myself and came at her with the broom handle.

The sharp end plunged directly into her middle. I kicked out against her chest and pulled on the handle at the same time. The handle came out, bringing with it blood and stringy flesh. I brought it across her face like a baseball bat. The force of the blow was enough to knock her off balance, and with another kick, I sent her on her back to the ground.

"Forgive me," I said and plunged the sharp end of the stick into her eye. Her body twitched a couple times then lay still.

I stumbled back a few steps and couldn't believe how fast I had taken her down. For some strange reason, my heartache was gone. So was the confusion. Instead, I felt . . . nothing.

Just . . . nothing.

Who was I? What had I become?

I had to get out of there.

# 35
# On the Move Part Four

Telecom handheld transmission:

There was a small, one-foot-by-two window toward the ceiling of the laundry room. Glass, with a grate on the outside. I broke the glass with the same broomstick that—

Anyway, I smashed the window, then standing on the washing machine against the wall, used the broomstick as a kind of thin battering-ram, all the while pounding on its end with the dustpan until, after an hour, the screws holding the grate to the outside wall finally gave way. I squeezed through the opening, took one last look at Selena's body then ran.

The undead were gathered out front. I ran past them, and the few who tried stumbling after me didn't have a prayer.

Adrenaline propelled my legs. All I wanted was to leave Selena and that laundry room behind. But now, writing this to you, I would give anything to see her again. Yet I've already seen her, haven't I? How many times has she recently come into my life only to die a short time later? Can I expect her return again? Will I see her? Did I really see her?

I'm telling you, I don't know if all this stuff is in my head or if it's real. Maybe I'm laying in a gutter somewhere, suffering from a zombie bite and all these crazy hallucinations—even this journal—is some sort of side effect of whatever it is they carry that infects people and turns them into one of them.

Are the zombies even real?

Maybe I'm just a regular old lunatic in a regular old world? Maybe you're as crazy as I am, and we're sitting in a padded cell somewhere, sharing the same delusional fantasy?

Gotta clear my head.

Wish I had some alcohol.

Need sleep.

Need Selena.

Need . . . I don't know what I need anymore.

———

His name was Jay. I met him after I pummeled an undead old man after the creature tried to take a bite out of me. The old geezer still tried walking with his cane even though he didn't have the coordination anymore. It was his cane that I used to beat him to the ground and eventually shove *through* his rotting throat to sever his head.

Back on point: Jay. His name was Jay. He was black, tall, built like a basketball player. Now don't go accusing me of being racist or stereotypical or anything. I'm sorry, but that's just how he was. The best part was that he was *alive*. Real. A human. He was the first one I'd seen aside from Selena in so long that—and I really mean this part—I forgot what it was like to relate to a real flesh-and-blood guy again.

He wore a red T-shirt, black pants, and this pair of sneakers that were gleaming white with neon green. He must've just lifted them from somewhere because they were too clean to be anything but new. Regardless, the dude came out of nowhere right when I was sending the cane through the old man's neck. He tried to stop me before realizing the old man was a zombie. Instead, he just came up beside me, set his sight on him, crossed his arms and watched.

Jay's sitting across from me now in the alley as I'm transmitting this. I told him what happened, about how I had to escape my building. I didn't give him the lowdown on Selena. Only said someone I really cared about had just died. Jay told me I could cry about it if it made me feel any better.

I've only known the dude for maybe a half hour, maybe slightly more, but I got to admit it feels amazing to be with someone other than myself and other than someone who haunted my mind and heart for so long.

I almost feel normal, like things used to be. Must never forget, though. Must never forget things aren't normal, not here, and not even *out there*, outside this crazy hallucination, if that's what this is. Normal people don't live in padded cells.

Getting sidetracked. Starting to slip.

Jay's going to keep me grounded. I just know it.

———

We made it under the Maxworth Bridge. It's in an older part of town, there for folks who can't afford zipcars. That's fine. There're no social classes anymore anyways.

Jay and I walked here, each watching the other's back. He told me he comes from a family of thirteen kids. He's the second youngest and has eight brothers and four sisters. They're all dead; died pretty much right after this thing started. His family was so huge the house they had couldn't allow for a separate room for everyone. Most of his brothers and sisters bunked together. He bunked with his younger brother, Willim. Jay doesn't know which of his siblings got infected first, but soon his whole family was transformed and him and Willim had to split.

They survived on the street for a long time; several weeks, Jay said. But his brother died. I asked Jay what happened. He only smiled and said, "Stupid kid slipped off a catwalk and fell. Hit the ground. Busted his head open." At first, I thought Jay was crazy for smiling at the memory, but then I got it. Jay was happy his brother wasn't around to experience any of this and, in a way, controlled his own death instead of falling victim to one of the undead. Jay's religious, too. Says he doesn't mind Willim's gone. He says that one day, when the time is right, he's going to join Willim in the choir in the sky, and not only William, but his whole family.

Right now, we're under this bridge, zombie free. I don't know if it's God showing Jay favor or if we're just plain lucky, but we're getting a break. No running for our lives right now.

For the moment, I'm happy.

Jay's thinking about what we can do for dinner. I told him I had some food back at my place, but we agreed it'd be too dangerous to go back there after what happened, at least right now. Maybe a different day.

We'll figure something out, but if anybody's out there reading this and can get to us under the Maxworth Bridge in Comptropolis, we'd owe you one.

Is anybody out there?

Anybody?

# 36
# Under the Bridge

Telecom handheld transmission:

Again, I'm sending this from a wireless handheld device. Excuse any typos. Editing on this thing is difficult. Already tried. Anyway . . .

We're under the Maxworth Bridge, Jay and I. Dinner was . . . awful, plainly put. Know what we had? Earthworms. Friggin' earthworms! Jay said something about them being high in protein. Whatever. Though we both ate, I got the sneakin' suspicion he just wanted to see me eat worms. But better worms for food than being worm food itself. Can still feel them wiggling on my tongue, their fishy scent and rubbery shells filled with grainy, oozing flesh.

Jay's beside me, curled up on the ground, trying to get some sleep. I'm on the first watch. Was hoping we'd both be awake just for the sake of company, but I also realize it's better this way. At least for now. My hope is to get back to my place tomorrow. Doesn't make sense the zombies would linger there once they find the building empty.

I'm not going to talk about Selena this entry, in case you're wondering. If anything, my brain needs a break from her, though I think about her constantly.

The main thing now is: What's next? Can't live under a bridge like some troll. I'm thinking skipping town would be the best option. The problem with that is Comptropolis is huge and getting to the edge of the city on foot would take at least two days, walking about ten hours a day. Maybe even three days.

Right now, silence is on the air, the heartbeat of the city long dead. Just keeping my ears perked for feet sliding across the pavement.

I'd really like to know what started all this and why oh why the undead have to eat the living. What did we do to them?

Frak! Just hate sitting here hence my rambling. When I write these entries, it takes my mind off what's going on and off certain people. Sometimes I think that none of what I said makes any sense. Sometimes I think half of it is boring. But them's the breaks for you. You should at least be happy *someone* is writing *something* and that *somewhere* there's somebody alive who's taken the time to tell you what's going on in his life.

What's that? You want to be thrilled and chilled by reading this? Give me a break. You want thrills and chills, go stand in the street and wait for the first flesh-muncher to come along. No, seriously, wait for them. Then when they grab you, don't try to run until their teeth meet your skin. Then you can try and rip your arm away from them. There's your thrills and chills.

And that's precisely my point: the media has killed you. Do you hear me? *Killed* you, even worse than the undead have. Yeah, I'm serious. Whether in life or even in entertainment, you've been brainwashed into *expecting* certain things and when those things aren't delivered to you, you throw a temper tantrum. I'm glad that technology is almost dead. I'm glad we don't have ad feeds shoved down our throats twenty-four-seven like before. I'm glad the podcasts have silenced, that television has blinked out and even the blasted Internet is on its last legs. It's done nothing but made people lazy and spoon-fed instant gratification. Myself included. But at least I've made the choice to accept that life sucks, is hard, and doesn't satisfy me instantly. The zombies have at least taught me that much. So I'm writing this rant to you, hoping it'll strike a nerve and even though you might hate my guts right now, I'm all you got. At least, if you have some semblance of a heart.

Welcome to reality. Welcome to the place where there's no plot, no neat little endings, no climaxes—just one crazy ride where zombies walk, some nut from Comptropolis writes to you, and somewhere someone is listening.

Jay just farted in his sleep. Bet you didn't see that coming, huh?

What? That throw you for a loop?

My point exactly.

At the end of the day, we're all just trolls under a bridge. Look at yourself and you'll see what I'm saying is true.

Still waiting for you to come round under this bridge, by the way. But you probably won't. That'd demand effort.

# 37
# On the Way Home

Telecom handheld transmission:

Both Jay and I are sore this morning. Sleeping under a bridge will do that to you. No matter. We're just glad we're still alive. The worst that happened last night was the calls of the dead floating on the night air. That, and one of those sleeps where you're more dozing than actually sleeping.

So this is what went down since then.

"Hungry?" Jay asked.

I nodded, but said, "I ain't having worms for breakfast. Feels like they're still crawling around my gut."

"Well, food is on the B-list right now. Main thing is staying alive."

"That's an understatement."

"But a true one."

"I want to go home, see what the damage is."

Jay looked off toward the buildings in the distance. "Not sure they'd be gone by now."

"Let's head that way anyway and play it by ear. If we see too many of them, we run. If not, one step at a time. Cool?"

The way he shuffled on his feet told me he was reluctant, but I'm sure he knew as I did that we'd be better off indoors, some place familiar than out here in the open. "Fine. Let's go."

Jay and I walked at a casual pace, keeping against buildings and cars, trying our best to blend in with the scenery. If we saw one of the creatures, we'd freeze and hope it'd pass us by. There was this rickety old codger out by the baseball stadium with most of his legs rotted away. His limbs were like a series of toothpicks all glued together. It was amazing they kept him standing. He saw us and, with head tilted back at an angle, started stumbling toward us, his dead eyes fixed on us the whole time.

We picked up our pace. The old guy seemed to try and pick his up too. After a few stumbly steps, he must have realized he didn't have a chance at catching us so slowed down.

But still kept coming.

"Hope he doesn't follow us home," I said.

"We'll lose 'im."

I picked up a broken chunk of curb about the size of a hardball from the side of the road. I lightly tossed it between my hands as we walked, every so often glancing over my shoulder at the old guy shambling behind us. Soon he was joined by a pale-skinned Goth chick with bright red hair, the lower half of her jaw missing.

"Cute," Jay said.

"If she wasn't dead."

"Still cute."

I gave him a wry glance.

"What?" he said. "A man's still got needs."

"Are you kidding me?"

We quickened our steps. Unarmed aside from the piece of curb, I didn't want to go toe-to-toe with the undead unless I had to.

At the street corner, I checked around the bend. A couple more undead milled about. I checked the other way. Same thing. Going straight would take us out of our way, and there were a couple zombies off in the distance anyway.

"Better make a choice, man," Jay said.

"We go right," I said, and readied the piece of curb in my hand.

As we went down the street, the couple undead that were there started toward us.

"Keep moving," I said.

"Duh."

More zombies started in down the street up ahead.

Jay growled and shouted, "That's it!" The boom of his voice sent a jolt through my ribcage and launched my heart into a panic. He ran toward the undead, waving his arms and screaming like a banshee. He didn't touch them, but kept several feet away, all the while yelling at the top of his lungs and jumping up and down on the pavement.

No response.

"They don't care!" I called after him, the whole thing setting me on edge.

Still screaming, Jay took a swing at the dead businessman to his left, socking the guy in the head.

"Great," I muttered and tore off after him. *Idiot.*

Arm cocked, I hurled the chunk of curb at the blonde, anorexic-looking chick coming up on the side. The curb struck her in the forehead, bounced off, and left a splat of blood in its wake. She dropped to her knees, eyes fixed forward, and fell over.

I grabbed Jay by the shoulders as he kicked the business zombie in the nuts.

"We've got to go!" I said.

The blonde crawled on the ground toward us.

"AAAHHHHH!" Jay's scream rang in my ears as I steered him away from the two undead.

We bolted down the next street and, now familiar with my surroundings, led him in a beeline to my place.

At one point, I had to stop and throw up, my gut hurt so bad from the stitch in my side. Warm, brown mush hit the pavement. Worms from the night before.

"You all right?" Jay asked.

"Yeah," I said, catching my breath. "Just sick of running."

"Me, too." He took me by the arm. "Come on, let's go."

As we walked down the street, a tingle came over me. Something was wrong. I glanced over my shoulder and there, heading into an alley across the way, was Selena.

I grabbed Jay. "Wait."

"What?"

Selena had already gone into the alley. I didn't know if I should go after her or if I was hallucinating or what.

"What?" Jay said again. "What did you see?"

I exhaled a slow sigh. "Thought I saw someone I knew."

"Unlikely." He tugged on my arm again. "We're leaving. Tell me which way to go."

I went with him, all the while periodically checking over my shoulder to see if Selena would come out of that alley. How many times was that now that I saw her, killed her, saw her come back, saw her die, saw her in a group of zombies—I've lost count to tell you the truth.

Something's seriously wrong, either with me or with her or maybe even both. I couldn't tell Jay about her living and dying yet. I still needed to figure it out for myself. What was certain, though, was I was running out of time.

My sanity was going quickly.

# 38
# Panic Attack

My apartment building was clear except for a couple zombies lingering in the hallways. Jay and I decided it best to just motor on past them and get to my suite as fast as we could. When we got to my suite's door, we counted to three then opened it, ready for the dead to come out, mouths open, arms outstretched. Instead, we found the place deserted and everything a mess.

The couch cushions were off and on the floor. My kitchen table was turned over, likewise with a couple of chairs. My clothes, dishes, and garbage littered the floor like a second carpet.

I checked for my computer. It was on the floor, the laptop's monitor nearly snapped off its hinge. I'm writing to you on it now. Still have the telecom handheld unit, though.

Jay and I paced the apartment several times, checking and re-checking for any undead that might be hiding. The closets were empty. The few items that remained in the cupboards were on the floor, nothing else within.

"Disgusting," Jay said as he lifted up his foot and showed me the crap on the bottom of his shoe.

As if seeing it suddenly triggered my senses, the stench of the dead and the funk they brought with them pierced my nostrils. I gagged and had to hold myself back from throwing up.

"Nasty," I said. "Wonder if I should even bother cleaning it up?"

"You kidding me?"

"Don't want to touch the stuff."

"You're going to have to if we're going to stay here."

"What are you talking about? It's my apartment, my call."

"Yo, man, I ain't stickin' around with poop and blood and who knows what else all over the place."

"You want to touch it, be my guest." I left the room and went to my bedroom. I sat on the edge of my bed and put my head into my hands.

Heart pounding, a sharp pain spiking through it over and over, it was hard to catch my breath.

So much happening. So much *has* happened.

Concentrating as best I could, I worked on slowing my breathing, my lungs and ribs feeling as if a boa constrictor was squeezing me.

Decisions needed to be made. I was tired of running. Tired of sitting here typing and whining about my life and Selena.

If Jay was anything right now, he was my anchor and a reminder of what interaction with real live human beings was all about.

The sound of shuffling objects came from the other room. I assumed Jay was cleaning up.

*Should probably go help him*, I thought.

When I stood from the bed, it was as if a fresh pair of arms wrapped around me anew and every breath was shallow. I was on my knees before I knew it, my chest aching, heart throbbing. Heart attack? No numbness in my left arm and, from what I'd heard, a heart attack is supposed to feel like someone is sitting on your chest. That wasn't the case here. There was no pressure against my chest; it was just hard to breathe, each sip of air I took was quick and shallow.

I was going to call out to Jay for help, but I could

barely speak.

What was I so afraid of? Had I just taken everything on the chin until now and suddenly my body decided to feel the pain of those blows all at once? I'd been through worse situations than coming home to a zombie-wrecked apartment. Why now?

Above the humming in my ears, Jay screamed from the other room. "Nononononono . . . . No way! Get out now! Nuh-uh. Not you!"

I crawled on my hands and knees to my bedroom door, then flopped myself out onto the hallway floor.

If I thought I already had trouble breathing, it got even harder because Selena just stepped through my apartment door.

"Stay back! Get out of here!" Jay yelled at her.

*He saw her,* I thought. *That means she* is *real. I'm not crazy.*

"Who are you?" she asked. "Where's Marty?"

"Marty? You know him?" Jay yelped. "I can't even believe I'm talking to you."

Selena turned around and saw me. "Marty!" She ran down the hallway and got on her knees beside me. "What's going on? Marty, what's wrong?"

"Can't . . . bre . . . breathe . . ." I said. It was so good to see her again, and despite the panic attack, her being there brought me peace.

"Here, sit up." She got her arms underneath me, and I put my own strength into it as she helped me up. She put her hands on mine. "You got to stay still. Calm down."

"Dude, don't touch her!" Jay said.

"Wh-what?"

"What's wrong with you!" Selena screamed.

Jay rushed over to her, arm and palm held out at his side like a hockey stick. When he got up to her, he smacked her across the head.

"Jay!" I coughed. Each breath pumped in and out at a rapid rate. Light-headed, green rimming my vision, I forced myself to get up and pull Jay off of Selena right before he was about to bring his fist down on her head.

"Stop . . ." When I spoke, it was barely a whisper.

"You don't want this, man," Jay said.

"Don't . . . I . . . I love her."

He stared at me a moment then rolled his eyes.

Selena looked at me as if she couldn't believe what I just said yet her eyes conveyed a sense of surprise instead of anger or disappointment.

"She'll kill you," Jay said.

*She already had,* I thought. *How many times is that now?* "Need . . . to . . ." The last thing I remember was my legs giving out beneath me.

# 39
# The Disappearing-Reappearing Girl

When I came to, I was lying on the kitchen floor. Jay stood over me. To my right, Selena was tied to a chair, hands and body bound with stato-rope. Streaks ran down her pale cheeks.

It broke my heart to know she had been crying.

"Jay . . ." I managed then had to take a deep breath. What I really wanted to say was, "I'll kill you."

Jay held out his hand and helped me up. The moment I got to my feet, a sharp pulse of pain blossomed at the base of my skull. My temples ached and my kitchen went fuzzy.

"Just chill out, dude," Jay said. "You hit the ground pretty hard."

I rubbed my head. "Yeah, you sent me there." I didn't know if I should pop him one first *then* rescue Selena, or simply go after the girl.

My sweetheart looked at me, her eyes pleading for help.

"You son of a—" Before I could finish, my fist snapped out and caught Jay square on the jaw. He fell back against the counter. I grabbed him by the collar of his shirt, threw him by the kitchen door, then slammed him into the wall beside the fridge. I leaned into him hard, pressing my forearm into his neck.

His eyes already began to bulge out of their sockets. When he spoke, his voice was rough and squeaky.

"She's . . . dangerous. Don't . . . trust . . . you have to . . . please . . . let me . . . breathe."

I glanced over at Selena. "Don't kill him but give him one for me."

I nodded and punched Jay in the gut with my free hand. I let go of him, and he slumped to the floor.

"See . . ." he said, coughing. "She's dangerous."

I opened the drawer next to me and pulled out a steak knife, then immediately got to work loosening Selena's bonds.

The moment she was free, she stood, marched over to Jay and kicked him in the head. "Bastard!"

She recoiled into my arms. Violence wasn't her thing.

"It's okay," I said softly. "I'll send him on his way." I took her face in my hands. "Are you okay?"

She nodded, sniffled, then said, "I'll live."

Jay held out a hand. "Wait." He coughed. "I'm trying to help you."

"Then you can explain to me what you were doing tying her up and knocking me to the ground." I looked at my knife, making sure Jay saw me do so. "Don't think I wouldn't."

"Just hear me out," he said, and carefully got to his feet. He held out his hands in front of him in a seeming gesture of trust.

"Marty, who is this guy?" Selena asked.

"Someone I met while trying to outrun the undead. How do you know him?"

"I don't."

"He sure acts like you do. Ex-boyfriend?"

She wrinkled her nose. "As if."

"Better start talking, Jay. I'm giving you ten . . . then I'm throwing you out."

"Her" —he pointed at Selena— "I've seen her before."

"So?"

"No, you don't get it. I've *seen* her, man. Outside, on the street. She walks with the dead. Sometimes she's all nice and pretty, like she is now. Other times she barely has a face left. But I recognize those eyes. I've seen her at least a dozen times. I've seen her . . . eat."

I took a step closer, but Selena jerked me back to my place.

"He's not worth it," she said. "Just get him out of here."

"Please, Marty, I'm telling the truth." Jay's eyes were wide, sincere.

I didn't know what to believe. How was it possible that he'd "seen" her a dozen or so times?

*But I've seen her several times, sometimes like this, sometimes deadly. She dies, comes back, dies, comes back,* I thought.

I turned to Selena. "I don't know what to say, baby."

"I do," she said. "Give me the knife."

I lifted the hand with the knife high up so she couldn't reach it.

"Give me the knife, Marty."

"No."

"Now!"

"No."

She walked toward me. I backed into Jay. Instead of attacking me, he caught me and helped me stand up straight again.

He leaned over my shoulder. "She's dangerous, man." He pulled my arm with the knife down. "Come on, do it. Just end her before she eats us."

"She's not a zombie," I said then looked at Selena: "You're not, are you?"

"No, of course not! How could you even say—you know what? I was a fool to come here. Forget it. I'm done. I'm leaving."

Selena turned around and took the other way out of the kitchen.

I blocked her before she could get to the main door. "Wait."

"No."

"Jay?"

"Yeah?" he said.

"Get out."

"Fine, man, whatever." He went past us and opened the door. Before he left, he pointed at me and said, "You'll be dead by morning."

# 40
# Two Bodies

Selena was on the couch, lying on her side, her legs on my lap. I sat there massaging her feet as she slept, thinking to myself how beautiful she was.

"Why'd you come looking for me?" I asked quietly, not wanting to wake her. "Out of everyone else, you came here." For a moment, I forgot I was looking at someone who had the uncanny ability to die and come back to life over and over. "Why you, sweetie? Why you?" *Why me?* "I always dreamed you and I would be together again. Just couldn't have imagined it'd be in a world like this and that you, of all people, would tear me apart like you have. I've lost you so many times I've lost count. Are you real?" I sighed. "I know you are. Jay saw you too. So it's not just me. But what are you? You can't be one of . . . one of the dead because they don't come back to life once they're killed. They don't come back beautiful and pure like you do."

Selena quivered. I put the back of my hand against the skin of her arm, thinking she might be cold. Instead, her skin was warm, but I thought maybe I should get her a blanket anyway.

Just as I moved to stand and place her feet on the couch cushion, she said, "No. Not . . . don't . . ."

"Selena?"

"I SAID NO!" With a yell, she jerked awake, sat upright, and stared straight ahead, breathing in and out good and hard.

"Hey," I said softly, and reached out to her. The

134

moment I touched her shoulder, she screamed and bolted up from the couch so fast my own heart jumped into panic mode.

She stood there, frozen, staring at me.

We stood there together, and I waited for the moment to pass.

Selena took a deep breath and exhaled slowly. "I'm sorry. I'm sorry. Just had a bad dream."

*Bad dream?* I thought. I've heard this before. From *her*.

"Do you want to talk about it?" I asked.

She put her hands on her hips and steadily breathed in and out. "So real," she said to herself.

I had to know. Was just she prone to nightmares or was this something else? She never said anything while we dated. "Tell me."

She sat back down on the couch. I sat beside her. Gently, I placed my hand on her back and rubbed it. "It's okay. If you want to talk, I'm here."

"So real," she said again. Then, "It was dark. Some kind of hallway with silver walls. Silver floors and ceiling too. Had it not been so dark, I'm sure it would have been beautiful. The air had this lemon-like scent, but also this funky stench of garbage.

"There were footsteps, Marty. Soft ones that dragged on the ground. At the other end of the hallway was a humanoid shadow. The way it held itself—it had to be dead, you know, like those things? I ran when it started moving toward me. No matter how fast I ran, it was like the creature was able to keep pace despite how horribly it moved.

"Then the sounds started, the calls of the undead as their moans filled the hallway. When I looked to see where the sounds came from, a pack of girl zombies were not far behind, twenty or thirty feet. All dark hair and pale skin. They didn't seem too decayed or rotten, but their jerky movements and shuffling feet were enough to tell me they were the undead as well. I kept running through the halls, all that silver making one hallway look like the next. No way out. Then the undead grabbed me and pulled me to the ground. Immediately they crouched down around me and clawed at my hospital gown. Once they tore through that, they started digging into me with their fingers. Eventually they broke through my skin . . . and started into my flesh. Blood gushed out, spraying me, then . . . everything. Their blood-soaked hands pulled out my stomach, intestines, kidneys—all that was within me."

*The same dream, the one she had before when she came here.* I couldn't forget it. Not when it scared her so much. Not a dream where my baby was killed.

"You're safe here," I said not really believing it myself. The undead had come here before. Who was to say they wouldn't again?

"I'm scared, Marty," she said.

"You're safe." I put my arm fully around her and squeezed her gently. She lay her head on my shoulder. A moment later, she reached around the front of me and wrapped her arms around me. The way she held me in her arms, so tight, so sure—I felt her shake as I returned the embrace.

"Everything's going to be okay," I said. "I've got you."

She just squeezed me tighter.

A flurry of emotions ran through me, and I didn't know if this embrace was solely because of the dream or because maybe—just maybe—she still cared about me.

*Why*— "—are you doing this?" I didn't mean for the words to come out.

"Hm?"

"Nothing."

She held me tighter. I adjusted my body and brought her as close to me as I possibly could. Her body fit perfectly into mine, as if my frame was carved out in such a way to accommodate only her.

When she pulled away, she looked at my face, a hint of uncertainty in her eyes.

Then she leaned in and kissed me.

At first, I didn't reciprocate, but instead just let the feeling of her lips against my own finish sending a bolt of lightning into my heart.

She moved back and her lips left mine. "I'm sorry," she said.

"It's okay," I whispered.

Her arms were still around me. She looked at me again then fell into me, our lips meeting again. This time I didn't hold back but instead poured out my love for her as our lips moved across each other's, our tongues gently touching then backing away, meeting and moving. She held me so tight it was as if she had never hugged anyone else in her life and only now was discovering the power of an embrace.

I didn't care. I needed her. All the time we had spent apart began to fade away like a bad dream. Our lips never left each other's, and even as she began to slowly undress, we still kissed. I followed her lead and began to remove my clothing as well, my heart pumping so quickly I got lightheaded.

Our naked bodies met, fit into the other's, and though I wanted to open my eyes so I could appreciate her beauty, I couldn't. So lost in her passion, I just let myself and my heart sink into her.

We made love on the couch; it was like we'd never been apart. Together, we shook with each tender movement, each reveal and each moan. I kissed her all over, and she did the same to me. It was like the first time we did this. Why here or why now, I didn't know. Maybe she just needed to feel loved? Maybe she was so scared, and I was able to offer enough sense of security she simply lost herself in the moment.

Maybe she still loved me.

Time lost its meaning, and her and I came together several times throughout the night. Out of respect for Selena, I won't write every detail, but the rest of the world faded away. There was only us, love, and a joy I thought I'd never feel again.

After, lying in each other's arms, I could only manage three words: "I love you."

# 41
# A Perfect Night Gone to Hell

Have you ever watched someone sleep? Have you ever taken the time, or are you too focused on your own fatigue?

Selena captivated me that night the way she lay perfectly still beside me, mouth slightly open, her eyes closed. I imagined a strange world of dream and thought dancing before her vision, full of secrets known only to herself.

She had the blanket right up to her chin, only her head peeking out, the rhythmic rise and fall of her chest a balm to my aching heart.

We've been here before, both before the undead plague and after. I've seen her sleep many times, wondering if she's resting comfortably or if she's merely dozing. Wondering if there's peace inside her or if sleep was her escape from this wretched world filled with the undead.

I could watch her forever but, I admit, a part of me wanted to wake her. Every moment she spent in sleep's embrace meant one less moment with me, and moments with Selena were always precious, especially these days.

I gently kissed her forehead then placed my lips upon hers. Even though she didn't return the affection, there was still an electric tingle when our lips met.

"Good night, princess," I whispered and lay down my head beside hers. I looked her over one last time then closed my eyes.

All was dark. No dreams came, none that I could

recall.

When I awoke, it was still dark and a tired headache hovered behind my eyes. My body ached to reach over and hug Selena and fall asleep pressed against her. I looked over. She wasn't beside me.

*Probably gone to the bathroom,* I thought. I closed my eyes, thinking she'd come back to bed any moment.

I don't know how much time passed, but I was jolted out of my sleepy haze by low, gurgling gasps and ear-splitting coughing. I bounded out of bed and followed the noise and made a beeline for the bathroom. I started to shake immediately upon seeing her. Selena knelt before the toilet, naked, blood and partly-digested food smeared on the seat and the floor around her. Her body shook with each gut-based lurch. A splash of red throw-up gushed from her mouth; half landed in the toilet, the rest running down her chin and chest.

If this was the old days, I would have called 9-1-1 immediately. These days, there was no one to call.

Heart galloping, I grabbed the towel off the rack and draped it over her shoulders and pressed my hand to her back. Her body shook beneath my touch then lurched as another gob of blood and stomach fluid burst from between her lips.

"Let it out," I said, not sure if that was even good advice.

Right after I said that, she started dry-heaving, her body rising high then settling low as everything within her locked and nothing came out of her mouth. It kept happening, and she gasped for breath, but she couldn't get air into her system.

"Come on, Selena, breathe," I said, patting her back, thinking maybe my effort would somehow shake something loose.

Her whole body quaked as it locked up again, her eyes wide behind the sweaty and blood-coated bangs dangling above them. It looked like she wanted to speak but didn't have the strength to say anything.

"Talk," I said. "Scream, yell, burp—Anything! Breathe!"

She kneeled there, frozen, not a single muscle moving. Her body was like stone beneath my touch, every muscle taut and strained over her bones. More blood oozed from her mouth. She remained still, letting it run over her lips and onto the toilet and floor.

Everything was so tense she shook head to toe—then released and fell to the bathroom floor.

"Selena!" I brushed her hair away with my fingers, her face smeared with blood and puke.

She lay perfectly still, eyes closed, mouth slightly open—as if she was sleeping.

Except she wasn't. She wasn't breathing. I put my hand to her chest and confirmed my suspicion that her heart had stopped.

She was dead.

Again.

———

I sat just outside the bathroom door, Selena's towel-covered body not two feet from me. I needed the wall against my back to keep me from slumping over. I stared blankly at the wall across from me.

"Over and over and over again, I wish you were here, my sweet tender friend."

Don't know where I heard it but it seemed to fit. Every time I glanced over at the blood-soaked towel covering my ex-girlfriend's body, a wave of electric emotion ran through me, the kind filled with numb-struck awe, hate, and frustration. Longing and pain.

"Over and over and over again, I wish you were here, my sweet tender friend."

*A perfect night gone to hell. Imagine a world where all is well.* "Tell me again, Selena, my dear, tell me why you've left me here."

The rhymes somehow helped me think even though they were awful. This wasn't a poetry contest.

Just couldn't believe I lost her again.

And even when her body stirred beneath the towel, I wasn't surprised.

Jay's words from before came back to haunt me: *You'll be dead by morning.*

# 42
# No More, I'm Done

I was up against the fridge, lodged between Selena's undead corpse and the fridge itself. For a second, I thought of somehow throwing open the fridge door, ripping out the shelves, then going in and holding it closed from the inside and hiding from her.

That's right. You guessed it.

Selena came back from the dead.

Again.

Her body was pressed against mine with such pressure that I wondered where she got the strength from. Was her undead form just instinct and muscle and that's where all its energy was channeled? Didn't matter. Her face was against mine, sallow skin, eyes drooping as if she was having a heck of a time trying to keep them open. If it wasn't for the coolness of her skin, you'd just think she was under the weather and that's all.

Studying my face as if trying to figure out who I was, Selena ran her dead hands up my chest, by my neck, then down my shoulders as if trying to seduce me into letting her bite me. Her touch was awkward, and though she had been dead and resurrected for several minutes at this point, I was still happy she was in front of me, her hands touching me.

I'm a sick bastard.

She opened her mouth and drew her face close to mine. I shoved her against the counter behind her. There wasn't much room, and she moved back all of one step before bending backward over the counter and hitting her head against the cupboard just above that. I slipped to the side and left the kitchen and went to the living room.

With a groan, Selena followed, her feet stumbling across the floor, this undead version of herself seeming to have some real trouble with maintaining her balance.

She stepped toward me, feet turned inward, one in front of the other, and reached out with her hands.

I pushed them down and moved to the side. She turned, keeping her body in line with mine. The hunger for flesh was taking over, I knew.

"Selena, honey, you can't do this," I said.

I could imagine her asking, *Why?*

"Because I don't want to hurt you."

*Good. Just let me bite you and we can be together.*

It was tempting, I admit, but obviously there was no conscious awareness of what was going on behind her gaze, so even if I became like her, we wouldn't be aware of each other *in that special way* anyway.

Sidestepping again, I added, "Please. I've hurt you enough. Don't make me do it."

*I'm going to hurt you.*

"No," I said and turned toward the door. No more. I was going to run, leave her, and never hurt her again. Except she grabbed me from behind, tugged me down and back, causing my legs to bend and for my head to angle upward. Selena held me tight, opened her mouth, and tried to bite my face again.

"No!" I screamed and flailed my arms, knocking her head to the side.

She let go of me; I lost my balance and fell, my back hitting the floor. A jolt of tingly pain shot through my shoulder blades and into my lower back. It quickly faded to an ache and I got up as quickly as I could, hearing something in my back pop as I did, a sharp pain running from the top right of my shoulder blade to the center of my back.

I headed for the door. Opened it. Selena hit me from behind, slamming me into the door. It hammered shut, my fingers getting caught between the heavy door and the jamb. Howling, I tried to yank my fingers out but they were stuck.

Selena grabbed me from behind again and tried to take a bite out of my shoulder on my free side. I shot my elbow up and caught her in the mouth. Her head snapped back. As fast as I could, I opened the door and withdrew my throbbing hand, the fingers feeling like someone was stomping on them good and hard with steel-toed boots.

I pulled the door open all the way and stepped out into the hallway. About to spin around and tug the door shut behind me, I ducked when a green glass bottle spun through the air straight at my head. It struck Selena in the face and she fell to the ground, jaded shards of broken glass sticking out from her forehead.

In the doorway of the suite across the hallway was Jay. He stood there holding the door open with one hand, the other resting on the jamb.

"Told ya, man," he said, "you'd be dead by morning."

I glanced over my shoulder. Selena sat up, glass sticking out of her head, blood running down her face in ribbons.

"Come on!" Jay said, waving me over.

Selena stood.

"I'm sorry," I told her, and ran toward Jay.

Selena grabbed me. I threw her against the hallway wall, ramming her head into the concrete, face first, jamming the glass into her skull all the way. She simply dropped to the ground and didn't move.

Shaky, I looked at her, mind and body racked with

adrenaline. I slowly went back to my apartment and closed the door and locked it.

I'd forgotten Jay was on the other side of that door, waiting for me to say something.

# 43
# Spam

It'd be nice if I had any booze left. No, check that, it'd be friggin' awesome! But, alas, here we are, dry as cold toast, just waiting for things to make sense.

After the big ordeal with Selena dying again, I just paced my apartment until my heels were sore all the while ignoring Jay's door banging and shouts in the hallway. Part of the time I heard him; part of it I didn't. Eventually I tired myself out so much I took a short nap right there on my living room floor. When I awoke, I got up, peed, then walked across the hallway to where Jay was staying. Pride told me to just forget about it, but I'm smarter than that.

Selena's body still lay there, a big shard of glass sticking out of her head. I looked away, unable to stomach it. Not for Selena.

I rapped on Jay's door. He opened it, didn't say anything, and let me in. You know you have a good friend when you act like a jerk and they take you back, no questions asked.

The suite he stayed in used to belong to this Spanish guy, Hernandez somebody. I never got to know him, not that he was all that friendly to begin with. Very much one of those people who only left their place just to go to work and get groceries. Come to think of it, I was pretty much like that too, because right now I can't say I knew my neighbours all that well despite living beside them for a few years.

"Any food kicking around here?" I asked after sitting

at the kitchen table for a few minutes.

"Found a can of spam, a couple packs of dried noodles," Jay replied.

"I'm not picky."

Jay got up from the table, pulled the can of spam from the cupboard above the sink, then rummaged around in one of the drawers and found a can opener.

"You don't need that, you know," I said. "There's a tab-key-thing on the side."

He picked up the can, tilted it left and right in his hand, then said, "What do I know? Never ate this stuff. Probably makes good spackle."

I chuckled. "Or window caulking."

He smiled and fiddled with the key on the can until he figured it out. He opened another cupboard and pulled out a plate then dumped the contents of the can onto it. After grabbing a couple forks from the drawer, he sat down, gave me one, and said, "Dinner is served."

"Beats nothing," I said.

Jay paused before eating, bowed his head and closed his eyes. Out of respect, I waited until he was done, then the two of us divvied up the spam. It was like half-dried baby food cut into chunks. We ate in silence—guys do that—and when we were done, Jay said, "Want to talk about it?"

*So much for forgive and forget*, I thought. "Not really."

"I'm not talking about us," he said. "The girl. Want to talk about it?"

I sighed. "There's not much to say." My eyes met his. "She's the love of my life, you know."

"I can tell."

I wrinkled my brow.

"I saw it in the way you looked at her, the way you defended her. No shame in that." He paused then added,

"But she's dangerous . . . or, at least, something's not right with her. Sorry to say that."

It was true. I didn't want to hear it, but Jay was right. There *was* something wrong with Selena. No one kept dying and coming back, not in the way she did.

"You said you've seen her before, yeah?" I said.

He nodded. "Lots of times while I was out and about. Sometimes she was downright pretty, even normal-looking except for a mouth covered in—" He made a circular motion with his hand in front of his lips. "Other times . . . other times the only thing that gave her away was her eyes. Eyes don't change. They're beautiful and easy to pick out."

"Yeah . . ."

"It doesn't make sense, though," he said.

I mulled over his words for a moment. "Something's up. Something weird. She's come here several times now. She's also died several times."

He simply looked at me, his expression reading: *Obviously. Tell me something I don't know.*

"Okay," I said, "have you seen anyone else? I mean, anyone else repeatedly who looked different each time? I don't go out much, but so far as I know, I haven't seen any familiar faces."

"Hard to say. Big city. But for me, no, she's the only one I've noticed."

"So, what, she's either got a pile of twin sisters or she's regenerating somehow or . . ." I didn't know what I was saying. None of it made sense.

"When you were together, was she, you know, normal?"

"Yeah. Of course. Everything was normal back then."

"Family? Sisters?"

"Nothing that would indicate a plethora of

look-alike siblings."

"Superpowers?"

"What?"

He was dead serious, which I didn't expect from him. "You know, some kind of special ability. Able to multiply herself or something?"

I couldn't help but chuckle. "If she did, she never told me."

"Just going through the possibilities."

"I know."

"And she keeps coming to you?"

"Yeah."

"Know why?"

"No. We broke up before all this started. The only thing I can guess is that everyone else she knows is dead or a walking corpse, and when we split, I promised her I'd always be there for her no matter what she needed. Maybe I'm her last resort?"

"Could be."

"And I'm fine with that," I said softly. "At least I get to see her."

He tapped his index finger on the tabletop. "We need a plan."

"For?" I coughed. "I mean, aside from the obvious shelter, food, and all that."

"What if she comes back?"

"Can't really stop that."

"No."

"Would you attack her again?"

"I don't know."

"I'll beat the hell out of you if you do."

His face went rigid.

"Sorry."

"No problem. I get it. But if she does come back, we

need a plan."

"I think what we need to do is figure out where she's been. She's come back in that gown, hospital coat thing." I nodded to myself. "Also a garbage bag, but yeah, that's our starting point. We'll find out where she's been then take it from there."

"And if she turns?"

"She's gotten sick first every time before now. We'll use that as our warning."

"Well" —Jay stood from the table— "you can stay here if you want or go back to your place."

It would have been nice to have company, but I needed some time to just stew and reflect. "Thanks, but I'll go home." I headed to the door. "Make a big fuss if you need anything."

"Sure."

I went into the hallway and closed the door behind me. My sweetheart's body lay by my door. Heart aching, I walked past it and into my apartment, tears in my eyes.

# 44
# The Hunt Begins

Telecom handheld transmission:

Jay and I headed out just after dawn. Normally, I'm not a morning person but I hardly slept last night, too busy thinking that maybe—just maybe—I might actually start making some headway on this whole Selena-sometimes-a-zombie-sometimes-not thing.

I'm writing this on the handheld as Jay and I walk around my neighbourhood, keeping our eyes peeled for Selena—or, Selena number 29 or whatever. We figure that if she kept coming to see me, there's no sense in going deep into the city to try and find her. If history is any guide, she'll come to us. Eventually.

As Jay and I walked around, he did most of the talking. Too much time by myself had wreaked significant havoc on my social skills. I could maintain a conversation, sure, but I'd much rather listen. Besides, I didn't think I'd have all that much to contribute anyway.

When we first left the apartment, the streets were fairly empty of the undead. A few stragglers stumbled about here and there, almost all several blocks away, so there was no real threat. As long as we kept our distance and our voices down, we weren't noticed. Until . . .

"See that?" Jay said.

"What?" I said and put the telecom away. (I'll finish this later if something happens.)

(Okay, picking up where I left off.) He pointed down the street, past a row of zipcars that had managed to line themselves perpendicular to the way they were supposed to be, plugging up the entire road. I followed his fingers only to see a row of the undead on either side of the zipcars, moving toward us single-file.

We both looked at each other and said, "Run!"

We turned to bolt in the other direction; more undead were headed our way, this group stretched the width of the road and up onto the sidewalks on either side, creating a barricade of rotted flesh and decayed skin.

Buildings lined us on either side.

We were boxed in.

Jay patted himself down, searching his pockets. "Got nothing useful," he said.

"Me neither." Man, I wished I had my razor-coated baseball bat.

The zombies drew closer.

"Can't stay here," I said.

"No kidding."

"You don't have anything?"

"Why you looking at me?"

"Just curious. Take it easy."

Jay patted his pockets again. "Got a lighter, a can-opener, and a pencil."

Not exactly a threatening arsenal.

We slowly backed up, the undead in front of us closer than the ones behind.

I tugged at the bottom of my shirt, nervous. Then I had an idea. "Gimme your pencil and lighter."

"Why?"

"Just do it!"

"Okay, okay." He handed them both over.

"Ever hear of a Molotov cocktail?"

Jay merely grinned.

"Follow my lead." I quickly jabbed the pencil through

the bottom of my shirt, just enough to get a hole started, then dug in my fingers and ripped a nice fat ring of fabric off the base. "I need you to keep them busy."

"How?"

"I don't know, but we need to get to those zipcars."

"Uh huh."

I took off, running toward the cars, heading straight for the undead.

"Hey, wait!" Jay shouted behind me.

*Thisiscrazythisiscrazy* . . . I thought. *Just keep moving. Don't give them anything to grab onto.* I weaved around the first zombie, shoved the second with my shoulder, then got up on the hood of a red zipcar before hopping down between it and another one. I scanned the sides of the vehicles, searching for its tank. A scraggily hag of a zombie with wrinkled skin and half her face missing started to squeeze in between the vehicles. I ran at her, kicked her down, then went back to the side of the vehicle. When I located the tank's hatch, I flicked it open and shoved one end of the piece of torn shirt in there, getting it good and wet with fuel. A pair of undead came in from the other side, both with arms stretched just ready to grab me. All I could do was back away from them, step on the old lady I just knocked to the ground, and use her to boost me onto the roof of the zipcar.

Jay was on the ground, a solid thirty feet away, doing jumping jacks and yelling, "Yo, over here! Hey, yeah, here, me! Come get it!"

Some of the undead took to his distraction; others stayed fixated on me.

I hopped to the next roof and then to another, getting some distance from the undead already climbing on top of the cars. As fast as I could, I crouched low, sheltered my fuel-dipped shirt rag from the wind, and lit the gas-run lighter beneath the cloth. It quickly went aflame and I had to hold my arm out to prevent getting burned.

*I should have kept that pencil,* I thought. *Crap. Lost it when tangling.* Could have used it as a miniature torch handle or something. The thing was hot. No duh. I know.

"Jay?"

"Yeah!" He suddenly shifted into high gear, sprinting away from the undead that had come right up to him. He dodged one and ran around another.

"I did this backwards. Need some help." *So should have just used my shirt as a wick or something.*

"What?"

"I said I need some help!" I jumped to the next roof. There, other undead were already in between the vehicles, their rotted hands reaching up to the zipcar's roof, grabbing for my ankles.

Jay was still running, his legs a blur beneath him. He was nearly at the end of the row of cars. Some undead hobbled after him. Others, it seemed, realized running wasn't their strength so turned around and headed toward me instead.

"Idiot," I said. The flame from the lit rag licked the inside of my wrist and forearm. I shouted from the sudden pain, dropped it, and was about to leave it when another idea hit me, one easier than the whole Molotov thing.

"You're crazy," I told myself, picked up the flaming rag and hopped to the next roof. I jumped two more and finally landed on one where the undead would have to catch up. My hand was beginning to burn but I didn't care. I had to get this done.

I jumped to the ground, opened the zipcar door, got in and waited, hoping my backup plan wouldn't kill me. It wasn't long before a zombie with greenish-gray skin started to climb into the car with me. I immediately threw the flaming rag under him. At first, nothing happened, and I thought he extinguished it, but a moment later a flame began to crawl over his tattered clothes. Soon, his flaming body lurched toward me, the inside of the vehicle suddenly hot. I backed up into the other door, opened it, and fell into the arms of a zombie waiting on the other side.

Where the heck was Jay?

The undead man grabbed me and held me in a tight bear hug. I spun on my heels and, shooting out my backside, was able to dump him onto his fiery friend. The two creatures cooked in the zipcar. I grabbed the nearest zombie and threw him into the mix for good measure before getting the heck out of there.

Zombies swarmed the cars: some in between them, others on the roofs.

I just ran like the dickens, sprinting to the furthest building, now a safe zone thanks to all the zombies crowding the vehicles. I scanned the street for Jay.

The roar of flame rose on the air as the wind kicked the fire to a whole new level and created an inferno.

I turned a corner. "Jay! You down here? Jay!"

Gasping for breath, my stomach swam and twisted in knots. I had to stop so leaned up against a wall and bent over, my head between my legs.

"It's okay, you're safe," I told myself. *Where's Jay?*

Catching my breath, I headed down the street, my throat dry and in desperate need of something to drink. A few zombies lumbered about, but none were close enough to be a threat just yet.

A hand touched my shoulder from behind.

It wasn't Jay's.

# 45
# Old School Comics



I swung around, lashing my fist out and connecting square with the creature's jaw. It was a bonehead move. Had I been off by even a couple millimeters, I could have easily snagged my knuckles on its teeth and probably would have gotten infected. The zombie shuffled back a step, paused, then stumbled toward me again, arms out.

My heart pounded—but not from fear. Only anger. These guys had caused so many problems and had hurt me personally by making Selena one of their own. Worse, making many Selenas one of their own.

The sound of shoes scraping against the sidewalk behind me forced me to reconsider decking the zombie in front of me. It was run or be killed. So I ran. I dodged around the nearest two undead, their hands rising into the air a second too late to grab onto me. Another I shoved to the side as I bolted down the sidewalk, hoping Jay was somewhere nearby.

*Don't go too far,* I thought. *We need to stay in the area. For now, anyway.*

I scanned the undead that were a block or block and a half away. None of them looked like my sweetheart.

A figure ran out from between a couple of fallen sky signs just ahead. A pack of zombies lumbered after him.

Jay.

"Hey!" I shouted, waving my arms and hoping he'd heard me. It didn't seem he did, because he kept running and disappeared between a pair of apartment buildings across the street, the zombies still after him.

But someone heard me. The undead in my nearest vicinity immediately set their rotten gaze in my direction and started toward me.

"Oh man . . ." I breathed. I glanced back over my shoulder and tried to come up with a plan. It seemed there was only one plan in this undead world: Run.

I took off further down the street, but a pack of zombies up and to my right saw me and joined their brethren in their mission to take me down.

A blur of color materialized on my left as I ran past an outlet store then quickly disappeared. I halted, turned, and headed back. It was a comics shop, the kind that still sold old paper copies of comic books that nowadays most people read on their eReaders and telecom units. Maybe they had a back room I could hide in? Maybe even a room with a lock on the door. Its large front window had been smashed during the riots when the zombie plague first hit. I stepped over the frame, my shoes crunching against the broken glass on the floor. Comics and old-school graphic novels littered the floor like a squirrel's nest, panels of Axiom-man, Superman, Captain America and others catching my eye as I stepped quickly through the shop and to the rear of the store. This was a place I had meant to go into back before all this chaos started. Interesting I was here now, looking to save my life amongst images of heroes that did it all the time.

A dented and overturned moneycomp lay on the counter to my left. Whoever smashed it up must have thought that because this place dealt in vintage comics, it must have dealt in vintage cash too. Idiots. Paper money and coins were phased out completely a good ten years ago if not longer.

Behind me, undead feet shuffled through the scraps of comics on the floor. A loud thunk made me look over my shoulder only to see one of the zombies—a much-decayed one—had tripped over the window frame and landed on its face.

I was already at the back of the tiny shop with nothing near me to use against them. Just a bunch of very old collectibles, some hanging on the wall behind me, others on the floor at my feet. Most of them were action figures. One was a Spider-Man web shooter for kids. There was a Superman costume, a plastic lightsaber, and a cap gun. I thought maybe I could get away with using the lightsaber, but its plastic handle was already cracked, presumably from whoever had been in here before me. There wasn't a back room.

Adrenaline kicked in and I wasn't sure if I was going to make it out this time.

The zombies drew closer.

I stepped on something, soft at first, but it gave way and my heel landed on something hard. I kicked at it through the scraps of comic pages covering it.

It was a sword. A fake one, but one that would still be dangerous regardless. Kind of. It was still in its black cardboard package, a red logo with what looked like a wild cat roaring, followed by silver letters reading: THUNDERCATS. Never heard of them.

I quickly bent down, picked up the sword and ripped it from its package. Crap. It *was* plastic; its gleaming silver paint job fooled me. But the plastic felt hard, solid.

Realizing how stupid this was, a brief note of hope still sounded in my heart. I lifted the blade and wound it back like a baseball bat.

The first zombie moved in.

I took a swing.

# 46
# Plastic Swords

Telecom handheld transmission:

The blade's hard plastic tip connected squarely with the zombie's temple, knocking his undead head to the side. It was enough of a distraction for him that I was able to push the creature to the side, get past him—only to be surrounded by three others: one in front, one to the left and another to the right. I kicked to the right, getting myself some distance from the closest undead. The one on the left grabbed me, her filthy hands and sharp nails digging into my arm. With a quick twist of the waist, I managed to bring the plastic sword across the head of the one in front of me. His flesh was so rotted around the neck the blow was enough to knock his head off his shoulders. Talk about a break.

The light coming in from the door to the shop was mostly covered in shadow, undead bodies blocking the sweet scene of the empty street beyond. The girl who held me on the left pulled my arm close to her mouth. With a shout, I jerked my arm free from her grip, felt a hot sting across my bicep, adrenaline quickly wiping the pain away. Like a madman, I swung the sword left and right, hacking my way through the undead like a safari guide plowing my way through the jungle. Of course, the blade didn't cut them down but was sturdy enough to send them a step to the side, buying me enough room to push my way past them to the street beyond.

A gunshot went off in the distance. I whirled around;

Jay sprinted toward me, lumbering zombies on his tail, something small and dark in his right hand.

When he caught up to me, he said, "I hate this." That was all. I think he was my new King of the Understatement.

"We gotta go," I said.

Jay squatted and dipped his head between his knees for a couple seconds, took a deep breath, then straightened. "God be with us."

"No kidding."

We ran down the street, the calls and moans of the dead rising behind us. A skyport was just off to the side down the next street. We headed there and hoped that folks had left a vehicle or two parked inside when the outbreak hit.

Each zombie that came our way, our first goal was simply to avoid them and run past. Except for the two near the skyport. The walls around the light gray, spiral-shaped garage were too high to climb. Two undead blocked the entrance, though I doubted they actual realized that's what they were doing.

Jay and I cautiously approached them, and when the dead old geezer with skin that flaked off his face like dry pastry saw me, he raised his arms and came right at me, moving much faster than expected. I wound up my sword, ready to hit him as hard as I could.

A loud *CRACK* echoed through the air, rocking my insides. The old man's head burst open at its top in a spray of blood and bone, and he fell to the ground. Another *CRACK* and a thud and the other undead dropped too. Jay stood by the one at his feet, raised his hand and showed me the gun.

"Where did you get that?" I asked.

"One of the dead had it. He got hold of me and as we

wrestled, I noticed he was once an Enforcer. Old school, if he's still using bullets. Could have been a ceremonial thing, for all I know. Doesn't matter. I noticed the gun in the holster so fought him to get my hands on it. Fortunately, it was still loaded. Blew his head off, too." He said that last bit with an unsettling grin.

"How many shots left?"

Jay cracked open the old revolver and checked the cylindrical chamber. "Two."

"Better keep them as a last resort then."

"Good idea."

More undead appeared down the street.

"Come on," I said.

We jogged into the skyport and began the long, winding ascent through the lot, looking for abandoned zipcars or skyvans. On the third level, we found an old hauler tucked in the corner. Haulers were kind of like large skyvans meant for families with too many kids. They were also used as repair vehicles around the city for skylights and hover signs.

Jay and I approached the vehicle with caution. He held the gun aloft; I had my sword ready and suddenly felt like a kid trailing his daddy on a hunt with a toy just so he felt like he could actually contribute something even though that wasn't true.

We kept our heads below the back windows, one of us on either side of the rear door. With a slight nod to each other, we peeked into the hauler's windows.

It was empty. But was it open?

Jay checked the handle. Locked. We each took a side of the hauler and checked the other doors.

All locked.

We met up again at the vehicle's rear.

"I need a break," Jay said.

"Me too."

There was only one thing to do then. I took the plastic sword and smacked it against the rear window. The sword bounced off.

"Nice," Jay said.

"Hope this Sword of Omens isn't trying to tell us anything."

"A 'Sword of What'?"

"Nothing."

With a quick flick of his arm, Jay used the gun to bust open one of the back windows. He reached in and unlocked the door from the inside.

We got in and closed the door and caught our breath in the dark. After a few minutes, my racing heart finally slowed and a sharp, heated sting ripped through my arm. I touched the skin and felt fresh blood on my fingers.

"Oh no," I said quietly.

Jay cleared his throat. "What?"

"They got me."

I touched the spongy, bloody spot on my arm. The wound was flesh-deep, an actual bite. I had hoped to God their teeth would have just grazed me, slightly scraping across the skin even if it drew blood.

But there was so much blood. Enough to know it was serious.

"Nonononono . . ." Jay said.

He tore the wide sleeve from his T-shirt and ripped the band again and made a makeshift tourniquet. He wrapped my wound tight. The stinging sensation along with the throbbing pain made me turn my head to the side and scream.

"Quiet, man, or they'll hear you," Jay said.

That prick. Didn't he know what I was going through? Just then a fresh pang of hurt pierced my heart.

I was doing this for Selena. The internal pain suddenly outweighed the external and the pulses of pain from the wound began to quiet down.

Selena.

This was her fault.

If it wasn't for her, I wouldn't have got bit . . . I wouldn't have . . .

"Argghh!" Jay screeched as he was pulled into a chokehold from behind by one of the undead, a grizzly man with gray skin, purple eye sockets, and a long, thick beard caked with blood.

Jay took hold of the creature's forearm, a futile effort to pull it away and have it release him. The zombie's head immediately went for Jay's neck. Its mouth opened wide and it clamped down on his throat.

Jay shrieked and his hands moved to where the undead's mouth met his neck. A spray of blood squirted like a fountain out of Jay's neck. The creature let go then put its big hands on either side of Jay's head. With brute force, he tilted Jay's head to the side and despite Jay's slapping his palms against the man's hands to stop him, the man bit down again, this time taking a mouthful of flesh, chewing while biting as if it hadn't eaten in days.

For some reason, my eyes were drawn to Jay's knees before they bent—weak—and his lower legs gave out from under him. The undead man held him as Jay slowly collapsed to the ground, his body going limp. The creature ate some more.

My friend was gone.

He was going to turn . . .

. . . and there was nothing I could do about it.

# 47
# It's all Coming Back to Me (Kind of)

Telecom handheld transmission:

As much as I wanted to run over to Jay's crumpled form, kneel down beside him and offer words of comfort before he passed, I couldn't. Not with the undead positioning himself one way then another over Jay's body, finding all the meaty parts to bite into.

My own legs turned to rubber and there was this thought I should do something . . . but I couldn't quite place it. Something to do with getting out of there, something—I felt a pulse of weakness shoot through my legs and it jogged my memory.

Run.

Just . . . run

So I ran. I made a beeline from the grisly sight of my newfound friend to a spot behind a blue zipcar. My heart raced but it didn't hurt. Wasn't the pounding kind of racing that was irritating, but rather like a water balloon slamming up against the inside of my ribcage then bouncing back off.

Fatigue washed over me and my eyes suddenly grew droopy.

The adrenaline was taking its toll.

Your body can only produce so much and put so much into your system before it needed time to replenish. Looked like my body decided to dump the adrenaline into my system in one powerful dose, leaving me full of energy yet, now, sitting here behind the zipcar, taking the opposite effect and draining me completely.

Must. Get. Up.

Easier said than done.

I took hold of the zipcar's bumper and pressed my palm against it, pushing myself upward. It felt like the heaviest squat lift of my life. But at least my legs were under me.

*Okay, just go,* I thought. I wanted to look back at Jay but knew it would only make matters worse. More undead will come to gorge on this newfound body. I couldn't stay here. And if I didn't look back at Jay, it would mean taking the loss with less anger and pain.

I hobbled at first, trying to find my stride. The hobble turned into a jog then into an all-out sprint. I didn't know where I was going. I just felt compelled to go in any direction: North, South, East, West or any variation thereof. I didn't know and I didn't care. Just dodged around zipcars and skyvans, leaping over half-eaten dead bodies, trying to ignore the funk on the air. I breathed through my mouth to minimize the smell.

Selena.

SelenaSelenaSelana.

"I need to get her home," I breathed as I rounded a corner. "Need to find her first."

*Home. Selena said she was at home. Why does that word somehow not fit the context of what's going on? Her apartment? Her parents'? A friend's? My place? Home.*

I ran, changing course with whatever direction felt right.

*She's out here right now. She has to be. Undead or not. Oh Selena, I'm coming. You might not want me to, but yet you came back to me in the beginning of this mess.* "Am I your home?"

The thought was uplifting, even brought a grin to my face. My heart sped up but not from the run.

It was love.

I loved her.

I so loved her.

One could argue it was bordering on obsession, but who—when they're truly in love—isn't obsessed with the other person? Do they not become a part of your world? Do they not *become* your world? Somehow, and I don't know how this works, but somehow they become your world, your life, your mind, your heart. Even your spirit. Life is actually *life* with them.

Without them . . . there is no life.

But Selena.

Selena.

My mind went blank, just a mass of black clouds when I mentally envisioned what I was thinking. There was . . . nothing. But the vibe . . . the vibe had Selena written all over it.

Something about her.

Something to do with all this.

Something with her living and dying and living and dying.

I saw her face. Her beautiful face. She gave me that smile of hers—mischievous but kind. That look in her eye, the one that said, "I know something you don't."

A woman of mystery.

A woman I loved.

Selena.

The woman I killed.

# 48
# What Have I Done?

Telecom handheld transmission:

"I didn't know how hot you wanted this, but I tried," I said to Selena. She was sitting on my couch, one leg bent on the cushion, the other hanging down to the floor. "I never let the kettle boil to maximum. Find that it's too hot afterward, then you gotta wait for it to cool enough to drink so I always cut it off early." I handed her her cup of hot chocolate.

She took it in both hands and gave it a smell. "Mmm, chocolatey."

"I've also been known to throw in an extra tablespoon above what the tin says to make it better."

"Won't be too sweet?"

"Nah. But your dopamine will give you an extra rush."

Her eyes lit up and she smiled. She took a sip, seemed to savor it, then pulled the mug away from her lips.

"Too sweet?" I asked.

She slightly shook her head. "No. Just right. Good. Sweet, yes, but not over the top. I like it."

She raised the mug to her lips for another sip and I did the same. It was then I noticed the large band-aid on the inside of her arm, just below the cuff line of her Britney Spears T-shirt.

"What happened?" I said, nodding in the direction of her arm.

"What?"

"To your arm. Scrape it?"

"No," she said quietly.

"Oh. Okay. Hope it's all right."

"Should be." Her voice didn't carry any confidence. Her tone almost seemed hopeless, but maybe that was just the way it came out?

We both sat there silently, sipping our hot chocolate, both every so often commenting on how thick and rich it was.

"You added cream, didn't you?" she said.

"It's the only way. Full-out cream. About a quarter of the mug. Adds a layer of richness but you can't really taste it."

"Smooth. I like it." She smiled.

Every time she smiled, I wished I could somehow take a mental picture and store it in a photographic memory. Except I didn't have one. Heck, my memory was spotty enough as it was. But memories of Selena—those stood out. Those replayed.

She set her mug down on the coffee table, folded her hands, and rested them on her lap.

I took a big swig of the hot chocolate then set my mug down as well.

We both stared at each other, each knowing what the other was thinking but not ready to act on it. Even after all this time being with her, I was still nervous to kiss her. I didn't want to come across as some stereotypical guy who was only in it for the physical. Though she knew me better than that and knew my kisses—each one—was my way of saying, "I love you."

She wrapped her arms around my neck, and my eyes drifted toward her band-aid. I was gonna ask her if she was sure she was all right again but thought it redundant so kept my mouth shut.

I put my hands around her waist and gave her sides a gentle squeeze.

She firmed her grip around my neck and pulled me in closer, about a foot away.

She just looked at me, as if analyzing me like a doctor. "What?" I said.

She smirked. "Nothing. Just looking at how handsome you are."

I didn't need a mirror to know I blushed. Heat filled my cheeks and my low self-esteem made me feel stupid. Here I was, me, some shmuck with this beautiful girl who was awesome both inside and out. She was just . . . her. Her looks, her mannerisms, her quirks, her voice and tone, that body. Selena wasn't perfect. I could pick out flaws as easily as the next guy, but those flaws meant nothing because her greatness outweighed her cons.

"You're the best, you know that?" I said.

"No," she whispered. "You're the best."

She leaned in and kissed me, her lips gentle against mine at first then she pulled me in hard and pressed her lips against mine before parting them and I felt her tongue gently lick mine. I returned the gesture and soon I was kissing her cheeks, her earlobe, making my way down her neck. I ran my hands up and down the side of her body, feeling her small frame and remembering how delicate she was.

At least on the outside.

Inside, she was a lion.

But a gentle one.

She began kissing my neck too. A kiss. A small lick. Another kiss, her lips hitting the nerves on my skin in just the right way. I hoped I was doing the same for her.

Selena stopped.

There was a pause and, at first, I thought she was just

catching her breath because sometimes kissing did that to you.

But the pause didn't stop. Oh no.

"What?" I asked, kissing her where her neck met her shoulder line.

I stopped and straightened. Her eyes were glazed over and dull, as if coated in chalk dust.

"Selena?"

She blankly stared off to something past me. I followed her gaze but there was nothing there but my front hallway.

"Selena?"

Was it just me or were her lips always purple?

"Hey." I gave her a careful shake. "Selena. Yo. Hey."

It was like nothing was registering upstairs. Was she having a seizure or about to? Did she have seizures but never told me?

"Selena? Selena!"

Nothing got her attention. She was somewhere else.

The color ran from her face. Something was wrong. It took a second but I realized I had to call for help. I didn't know what to do. If it was a seizure, you're supposed to—if possible—lie the person down and let it run its course.

I went to carefully lay her down on the couch, but her body was as rigid and immovable as stone.

"Selena! Wake up!" She didn't acknowledge me, and I discovered her chalky-white eyes anew.

Could she see me? What was she looking at?

She looked at me, arms still around my neck.

Her mouth opened and this awful smell like thick horse manure escaped her throat.

That wasn't chocolate.

Stomach trouble? Sick? Gas?

Quickly, her mouth was open and on my neck. I felt her teeth start to press against my flesh. This wasn't foreplay. This was no playful nibbling.

The teeth pressed harder; any harder and she'd bite me.

I shoved her away.

She lunged right back.

There was something wrong with her teeth. They looked normal, but each tooth seemed to have pronounced ridges, as if for cutting. Not vampire teeth. This was something else, something . . . different.

Selena went for my neck again. I shoved her away, and as I did, she grabbed my arm with both hands and opened wide. Her face headed right for by bicep. I managed to get my foot in between us. My foot pushing hard against her chest, I kicked her off.

I sprung off the couch and stood in front of her. "What're you doing!"

She came at me again, this time her skin paler, a light gray, ashen and dull.

"Selena!" I jumped back. The last thing I wanted to do was hurt her. Not Selena. Not my Selena. She could come at me with a gun and I still wouldn't raise a finger at her, but yet . . . I already had, hadn't I? I kicked her.

I kicked my girl.

How could I? What was I thinking? Some macho self-defense against a tiny girl? Some stupid male-hormone-driven instinct?

My chest went hollow, my heart in my gut. Head full of fog, wanting to punch myself in the face, I instead directed my fist toward her face when she lunged for me again. I popped her good in the mouth, but instead of shutting her mouth just as the hit was being delivered like most people would, she instead opened her mouth wide, and once again, her teeth scraped against my skin.

"SELENA!"

With a growl that could not have possibly come from my sweet baby, she dove right at me, collapsing onto me, using her light weight to her advantage. I lost my balance and she fell on top of me. She repeatedly plowed her face into my arms and chest; each time I pushed her away. I finally figured out this was no seizure. Some sort of schizophrenia? Multiple personality disorder? Even if those were true, it did not explain the changes to her appearance. It was like she died, before, there, on the couch, sitting.

But no one comes back from the dead.

"Selena! Get . . . off!" I kicked her away again and this time I ran for the door. Like I said, I couldn't hurt my poor baby even though it already got to that point. I thought about me, some jackass, punching her. If there was any chance of a future, that ended it.

She chased me as I headed for the door. Before I could open it, she slammed into me, pushing me into the wood. I hit my head. That stupid hollow thunk echoed in my brain.

I shoved her to the side and ran for the kitchen. I don't know why or what my reasoning was. The kitchen was a closed-off area.

She followed me into it in an instant, her eyes white and dusty, this girl . . . this girl I knew . . . she wasn't there at all. This was someone else. This was *something* else.

"S-Selena?" I kept my tone as soft as possible.

With a wild, gargled breath-like shriek she held out her hands as if to reach something only she could see then headed toward me quicker than I expected. There was hate in that blank gaze.

Hate coming from a loving person.

Hate for me.

*Go ahead, Selena,* I thought, *I deserve it.*

Deserve what, I didn't know.

She had my shoulders again, mouth open, her face expressionless. It's like she wasn't in control. Had I fallen in love with someone with some serious mental issues?

She went to bite down on my shoulder. I pushed away her head at the side and went for the counter. Selena turned toward me and came over, arms out again, mouth slack.

"Selena," I said firmly, "don't. Please don't. I don't wanna—please don't make me . . . please don't make me hurt you."

That awful stench came out of her mouth with every breath. The odd thing was, her chest wasn't expanding and contracting like she was breathing. It was as if all the air she had was contained in her throat and she was somehow able to breathe it in and breathe it out in shallow breaths.

I pushed her away.

That did it.

She came at me.

Hard.

The next moment . . . the next moment . . . I just, sorry, I can't say. I won't. It didn't really happen. It couldn't have. Not me. Not her. Not . . . no . . . something isn't right. It's this world of the undead that's clouding my memory, making me think or remember things that aren't true.

But I . . . I . . .

Oh, Selena.

———

To be honest, the rest is spotty. Like pieces of a dream. Sharp shards of memory or imagination or I don't know what—It's there, in my head. That cord. That toaster.

I grabbed it, the toaster. Two hands. Firm grip, fingers locked like claws on either side of the appliance.

The smell.

Her eyes.

Her teeth.

Her teeth were right up against my vision, her face nearly occupying all I could see.

The toaster.

My grip.

The adrenaline.

The awful sound of metal hitting bone when I swung the thing as hard as I could at her head.

It knocked her to the side, made her stumble. She righted herself, turned around to face me, and just as her mouth opened wider than a yawn, she got all but one inch closer and I smashed the toaster down on top of her head. The brute force of the blow made her drop to her knees.

I don't know what happened to me after that. Just flashes. Ideas. Thoughts of hitting her again with the toaster then somehow getting behind her and wrapping its cord around her neck like a noose. She hissed. Growled. Tried to turn her head to face me, that mouth of hers, the one I kissed so tenderly so often—it was looking for a target. I brought the toaster hard and fast across her face then tightened the cord around her neck.

I swear . . . I swear to you my plan was to simply cut off enough air so she'd pass out.

But Selena didn't.

I brought the toaster down on her head.

Over. And over.

# 49
# After



Telecom handheld transmission:

I came to and once the echoing in my ears stopped, I realized I was looking at my kitchen ceiling. Sweat made every clothing item I wore cling to me like a desperate child hugging its parent. Water in my eyes . . . but not tears. Maybe sweat.

No.

No.

It *was* tears.

I turned my head to the side and all I saw was this body, this female body that I did not recognize, attached to what could only be said as half a head. The back half. Her face . . . her face was gone. I leaned onto my elbow and looked over at her.

Selena.

There was no nose. No eyes. No mouth. Teeth were scattered around her head almost like a halo, as if on purpose.

Flesh—wide-open flesh—was her face. The gray skin was gone, and her cheekbones were dented and cracked. Blood leaked out of every crack in her facial muscles, every crevice of bone, every opening it could find.

Black blood.

Blood was dark, yes, but this was black, not a hint of red anywhere.

The bottom of the toaster was curved and dented. She still had the cord around her neck.

I did something.

Something awful.

I killed her.

No. No. Not me. I'm not a killer. I've only been in one scrap in my whole life where it was me or the other guy, and even then I didn't dismantle his face like I did Selena's.

Her body was perfectly still.

Empty eye sockets gazed at the ceiling, the goo of squashed eyeballs sitting in those sockets like raw egg whites in tiny cups.

My throat locked. There was a punch to my stomach, then my throat unleashed more puke than I ever thought possible. Over and over again, I lurched and lurched until I was drained dry, and even then, I kept going, dry-heaving, the gore of my girl making me die.

But I wasn't dying. This was worse.

In a split second, my heart started to race and I came back to reality.

This was it. This was real. This happened.

I killed someone.

I crawled along the kitchen floor and pulled myself onto my stomach in the hallway and lay with my face against the ground. I threw up again, this time a little coming out. I spat. Dry-heaved a couple times then choked on whatever little mucus there was until I was coughing like a madman trying to clear it.

My eyes watered but the tears . . . those were gone. All I could think about was what I just did. What bits I remembered doing.

My girl.

Dead.

Selena.

Don't go.

# 50
# A Muddled World

Telecom handheld transmission:


Jay was going to eat me. I had to lose him. Clenching my teeth, I got my feet strong and sturdy beneath me, mentally focusing my strength into my legs, feeling my muscles grow with power as I focused.

Run.

And I did. I ran. I ran so fast. The scenery around me changed like transitions in a dream. One moment the grungy wall of a building, the next zipping around the bumper of a vehicle, after that, some sort of glass and shards, then a sidewalk, then . . . then . . .

It was all "and thens" after that. A dream chase. But Jay, he wasn't behind me. Not anymore. There were others no doubt hunting me. Other dead pricks wanting to take me down.

I kept moving, heading southwest and not knowing why.

*I'm at home.* Selena's words from earlier came to me.

I ran. But her apartment was the other way. Home.

She was at home. Yeah, at home. Alive. Fine. Healthy. Well.

No, she couldn't be, and even if she was, she wouldn't stay that way forever. Selena kept turning into a zombie. Was she possessed? What about the others? Were they *all* possessed and Selena happened to be at the wrong place at the wrong time and was possessed, too?

I slowed to a stop and stood there, breathing heavy,

catching my breath. The funk of the dead lingered on the air and each gulp of air was like inhaling a bad cigar that'd been used by more than one person. Someone who completely ruined the tobacco by . . .

The ground spun in front of me and for a second, I thought I was going to pass out. I straightened, making sure my head and back and neck were all in proper posture. I let the wave of dizziness pass.

The fake bandage around my arm thanks to Jay was slowly getting damp.

I was going to become one of them soon. I didn't know what to expect or feel when I finally changed. Would I die *then* come back? Or would the transition be smooth. One moment alive, the next dead, the next undead. Or would I just become one of them like Selena did. She just changed that first time. Eyes all chalky and white. Her skin slowly growing paler and paler. Her lips turning purple. How long between the bite and the change was there?

There was no way to know or tell. I could be me, here, right now, but in a minute from now, I might not be me anymore. There might be no me. Just some bloodthirsty, flesh-eating monstrosity that used to cling to a girl that he lost over and over again.

And no one would ever know.

No one except you, reading this, if this story is even being read. I'm transmitting as best I can, I swear. I don't know what snippets you got or if you got the whole thing, but if you're reading this, the best thing you could do for me is find me . . . and kill me.

# 51
# I Just Don't Know Anymore

Telecom handheld transmission:

By the time I made it over the bridge, I was spent. More than exhausted. I was walking like one of *them*, dragging my feet, just trying to reach my destination except I didn't know what my destination was. Just something over there. Something southwest. Yeah, that direction. You know when you start walking without any real place to go and you wind up being drawn in a certain direction and you can't explain why. You just know that over *there* is where you oughtta be headed.

I hope it's not this bite. I hope it's not in my blood. I hope their spit and goo and phlegm and whatever else they have in their mouths isn't seeping into my bloodstream, tiny drop by tiny drop. But, I suppose, tiny drops were better than big ones.

I'm not ready to turn. To become one of them, to be the thing I hated with my heart and soul and gut and mind and entire being—I deserve it, don't I? I killed Selena. Not just once. Many times. But like all killers, there's always that first time. Like the saying goes, you never forget your first time. But I did forget. Blocked it out. And even when it started to come back, it wasn't wholly there. Just pieces of a nightmare that somehow made its way into Reality. Somehow made me hurt the girl who killed my heart. The girl I love despite that. The girl who I forgave and just simply wanted back. No strings attached. No making up for dumping me. No special favors or any demands.

All I want is her.

And I'm dying. Or I guess, *un*dying. But not to life. Undying unto death and into a birth of decay and hunger and blood.

My arm. It's starting to hurt. I want alcohol. Any kind. Just give it to me. Numb me. Change my headspace. Something.

Anything.

I hope I'm still transmitting. I plan to write as I walk, telling you what's going on. If you're reading this or listening to it somehow, please, come get me. I'm here.

No. Don't.

I might kill you if you do even if I haven't changed over completely yet.

I don't know how this works. I took a life. Took several lives. All belonging to one person. I don't deserve to be rescued. I don't deserve a cure if one has been found. I don't deserve people making me comfortable as I pass from this world back into it as something else.

Let me die on the street like a rabid dog that deserves to not belong to anyone for fear they might hurt them.

Let me die right here, right now. This sidewalk. Take me away. Show me Selena one last time then let me go.

No. Again, please don't. I mean, leave me be. Just don't show her to me. Don't let me see her again. She's too dangerous. *I'm* too dangerous.

My head. There's something wrong. Maybe I was the one with the mental issues? Maybe I was the one with the split personality? Maybe it's me who had this secret psycho side I didn't even know about until it showed up? Yeah. Maybe that's it. Split personality people don't know what their other selves are thinking. Maybe that's me. Maybe there's some murdering punk inside who is thinking of how to take the next life.

Maybe this whole thing, this whole story, all this stuff I've told you—maybe it's just me talking to myself. Maybe I'm in a padded room somewhere staring at the wall, trying to figure out what the hell happened and concocting some bizarre story of love and zombies. Maybe Selena is at the hospital now, looking at me through a pane of glass, wondering where I went, and there I am, staring blankly at a pillowed wall.

Maybe I finally broke.

There is no fix. There is no treatment.

Just me and my psychosis.

# 52
# Phantom Walk

Telecom handheld transmission:

My feet hurt. Each step on the stupid concrete feels like I'm slapping my foot down on one of those old shoe-cleaning brushes you had in your mudroom. The kind you scrape your boots on to get the mud off. Except it felt like I wasn't wearing any boots.

My arm. That bite. I feel its sting and ache and burning. I'm tempted to lift Jay's so-called band-aid and take a look for myself. Surely if I had been bitten deep it'd hurt way more. But that didn't matter. A shallow bite or a deep one—the outcome was the same. I can only hope it to be over quickly.

Drip.

Drip.

Drip.

Fatigue gripped the corners of my eyes and the strong weight of sleep pulsed behind my eyeballs, begging me to lie down, close my eyes, and just drift into darkness. This fog. This haze. I knew it. It was a friend. All those nights with the bottle. All those nights crying like some baby-like addict. Nothing but a head spinning, trying to figure out why everything sucked so bad.

Late-night walks, air that was supposed to be fresh only suffocating.

Selena had an aura. It emanated from her like this all-encompassing sphere that took me in. Those late-night walks—I was still in her sphere even though she was far away. Those walks had a feeling to them. A sensation of both love and pain. A hurt that ached my insides to the point I'd sometimes stop and just sit there on the sidewalk, lost, staring at the gray of the cement, hoping that I was in some kind of dream and I'd wake up any moment. But I also kind of liked those dreams.

I was still in her sphere.

I was in it now.

Walking. Arm hurting. My hand hanging by my side. My fingers were partially curled and there was this phantom sensation of holding something, something light. It hung off my fingers as much as it lay across them. There was a decent amount of it, whatever it was. But it wasn't pretty, that much I could tell you.

What was it?

My feet are really dragging now, and I'm tired of typing. No, must finish this journal. When I die—then undie—this record will be all that's left of me. Some kind of memory recording that may or may not be discovered. But if there was Jay, that means there might be others. I really doubt it was just Jay and I left alive in this stinking city. Then there's Selena. She's alive too. Kind of. She just needs to quit dying on me.

The thing I thought I had in my hand . . . it was there then it was gone.

Light. Kind of coarse. It was, or at least had been, wet at some point.

I envisioned walking along with Selena's dismembered hand in my own. I gave it a gentle squeeze and for a second, I felt the resistance and solidity of her flesh. Her hand in mine, just like it used to be.

The hand was gone now. So was the sensation of holding anything.

I kept on. Southwest. The sphere. It was still with me.

Do you understand? Sometimes I wonder if you even comprehend these metaphors, whoever you are.

Sorry. I don't mean to be rude. Just tired, broken, and upset.

And hurt.

Inside and out.

Plain old hurt.

I'm so tired.

It's back in my hand again. This thing. I look and all I see are my filthy fingers. A phantom image I can briefly see then it disappears. What was I holding? What *am* I holding? I look again. My hand is empty. I checked the other one just in case I've truly lost it and am looking at the wrong set of fingers. My other hand is empty too. I try my pockets as if searching those will help. It doesn't. Just thought maybe I put the thing away.

Shaking my head, I try and bring myself back to the present. Rattle the brain, so to speak. Give it a reboot.

No. No reboot. A solid eight hours of sleep would do it, but I ain't sleeping out here, and my place is now far away. Must trudge on.

Southwest.

That thing in my hand. So light but taking up so much space.

I rub my thumb along the imaginary item, an attempt to feel what might be there. What my *mind* is trying to put there. Some sort of dealing with trauma is going on and the timing couldn't be worse. Why here? Why out in the open? Why now does my brain want to deal with stuff?

It's in my hand.

It's Selena's hair.

# 53
# Falling Apart

Telecom handheld transmission:

All I could see was brown before my eyes, wisps of gorgeous ringlets caked and matted with blood. My hand was in front of my face, holding the hair to my eyes as if I was trying to make my eyes a microscope and absorb every detail of her hair. The tingling ache in my arm brought me around and I was face down on the sidewalk, Selena's hair in one hand, this stupid typing device in the other.

I must have passed out.

Or got bit and fell.

I checked myself over as best I could. Legs were intact, nothing missing. Torso, same. I felt around my neck and shoulders, even my cheeks, and found nothing. Just a head full of haze and a body that gave out on me. Too much stress might do that. Too much anxiety, especially with the shallow breathing and hyperventilating. I'm an idiot. If it was anxiety, sure, who could blame me? But even so, this sidewalk is no place for a run-of-the-mill human. I'm lucky nothing came along and . . . never mind. There they are, shuffling toward me, about a half dozen of them. They're about thirty feet off. If I hadn't come to when I had . . .

*Thank you, Selena,* I thought. Yeah. I typed that in italics so you know what I was thinking. Maybe she was being my guardian angel because an angel is what she is after all. That was corny. I don't care. It's true. Now buzz off.

Sorry. Just frustrated and angry.

Twenty feet now, the creatures.

I got up, didn't bother to dust myself off, and high-tailed it out of there. I didn't know where I was going but was still headed southwest.

Something was over there.

Some vibe of . . . of . . . I don't know what, but it was familiar. The direction, I mean. Long-lost familiar but familiar nonetheless.

I think they're gone, and by gone, I mean I can't see the undead anymore and must have lost them. They're not too bright, which is to anyone's advantage, but some seem smarter than others. Nothing close to genius or even normal, but some seem to have hung onto their humanity a little more tightly than others.

Were they aware of what they were doing? Did they notice their dragging footsteps? Did they notice their slack jaws and vacant gaze? Maybe the gaze told you everything.

Selena had that gaze—lost, out of place, some hint of confusion on an already-befuddled mind.

Selena.

Southwest.

Her sphere.

I'm coming, baby. I'm on my way.

I looked at my arm. Blood was starting to seep through Jay's bandage. I'm getting worse and I'm out here alone. I just don't know how it's going to feel when I turn. Nobody's ever said because, well, they can't. Only moan. Only groan. Only expel hot, funky air.

A jolt shot through my chest but was quickly subdued when I saw I still had Selena's hair in my hand. Thought I dropped it. But I'd never drop it, would I? I was too obsessed. Too driven. Too concerned about what happened to her.

What happened to this city.

What's happening to me.

Tell me. Please. Someone say something. Reply to this thing!

My hands shook. Excuse me. Need to just hold this thing for a while. Need to just walk and hold this record of life in a dead city.

I'll be back in a minute.

If I have a minute.

———

This typing unit—I don't know how long it's going to last. Are you seeing this? It got knocked to the ground. Hard. A group of them—the undead—jumped me. Well, "jumped" isn't the right word, but I was turning a corner and there they were. A swarm of them, their crowd at least six people deep, maybe three or four wide. That's around two dozen of them. I was two feet away. So were they.

I think I dropped Selena's hair.

Hands were on me, pawing and feeling like a dog pawing at a dead bird. Fingers found purchase and I remembered looking to my shoulder to see four chubby fingers holding onto me tight. I went to look at my other shoulder for some reason and it was then I was pulled in. That hand on my shoulder pulled at me and I was in a dream, the kind where you're trying to get away from something but can't.

An open mouth.

My fist.

My knuckles are red and blue now, hands covered in

blood.

I hit him. Punched him in the face, the throat, the center of his chest. He took the blows but kept drawing forward. The others joined in and soon I found myself surrounded by smelly, decaying bodies. Dirty clothes and gray skin. And the sound . . . even now I can still hear it. It was full of echo—subtle—but airy. The moans and gargled groans coming from their mouths reminded me of the same sound Selena made. But the *multitude* of airy voices.

Their weight started to press in on me and more hands found hold. A pressure on both my shoulders forced my knees to buckle and begin my descent to the ground. I gripped the typing unit hard. I thought of Selena's hair and knew my hand was empty.

Where'd it go? Who took it? Give it back!

With a screech, I held out my arms like helicopter blades and summoned all my strength into my legs, mentally fortifying them like pillars of oak. Another screech, this one inhuman and full of rage and panic. I righted myself so I was standing then spun in wild circles, my arms slamming into the creatures, some getting hit by my hands, others by my arms. It wasn't to defeat them. I had nothing to destroy their brain or remove their head. It was a space-giver.

It was a chance to run.

# 54
# Bird in a Sphere

Telecom handheld transmission:

Spinning, spinning, spinning—A madman who's had enough and was about to unleash hell. Every turn-around struck something: A face, a shoulder, the side of an arm. Anything to buy me some space and some time.

My hurricane of sheer adrenaline got me about a half a foot clearance all around. I dove at the zombie blocking my way out, tackling her to the ground. I struck her with my fist, punching her in the face over and over again, my hand trying to slug the cement behind her head *through* her head. That mouth was open. Bone on bone as knuckles met teeth. Then I realized if her teeth cut me, if something from her got inside—No, couldn't have that. I switched arms and wailed on her, this typing unit my sledgehammer, repeatedly pounding it down on her face, its edges tearing skin and revealing dead, purple-gray flesh beneath. The more flesh I exposed, the more excited I got at the prospect of finally beating her.

Killing her.

Ending her.

But the others came in, pushed against my back, forcing me to lay on top of her. I planted my hands on either side of her shoulders and did a push up, getting my knees under me then my legs and feet. I swung out— lashed out—screamed and struck a dead man across his skull before turning and screaming and running.

Tears blurred my vision, and I didn't know why I was

crying. I wasn't sad. I wasn't happy. I wasn't even panicked.

I think those tears were the acid memories of this dead world and everything that's happened since Selena came back. She played with my heart again. She made me kill her over and over.

Running. Typing. Are you getting this?

I looked up and was drawn slightly to the right.

Southwest.

I kept going.

The sensation of my legs moving hard beneath me left and I was floating, moving quickly toward who knew where.

Flight.

I need a drink. Ground me somehow.

Movement. Run. Southwest.

. . .

. . .

. . .

. . . and then I felt my legs again: Nothing but rubber.

Gasping for air, I started to slow down. No. Had to keep moving. But my body is saying otherwise. Ahh. I can't type and run at the same time. This is taking forever. Those last two sentences took me five minutes. More than that. Maybe less. Doesn't matter.

Hold on. I can't breathe.

. . .

. . .

Okay, fine. I'll stop. I'm at an intersection, four buildings that are as high as a pothead on weed. Can't see their roofs. Clouds in the way.

Sensations of Selena. Her sphere.

I've been here before.

# 55
# Spades



Telecom handheld transmission:

This is it. Something inside tells me that. The store sign is crooked but SPADES is spelled out loud and clear in black metal, bold lettering. It's actually in good shape considering all that's happened to this city.

Nice to see something put together and holding its ground.

Spades. A liquor mart.

I go in.

It's mostly empty. Empty of people, of course, even the dead, and the shelves are stripped bare except for a few bottles tipped over onto their sides, probably from a mad rush of looters looking to strip the joint before the living dead got to them.

Just show me a clear liquid. No, not water.

Tequila.

The good stuff.

The stuff that started this whole diatribe and whacky life of death and undeath and life and unlife. In my life, anyway.

The bottle has a crack but nothing is broken. I can't read it. It's in Spanish. I'll take that as a good sign.

Oh guys, this is so good. Need to slow down. I'm chugging the stuff. Thirsty. Hungry. My arm. The warmth of the booze makes its way down my throat and fills my chest with hot relaxation. It doesn't take long—mere moments—for my heart to stop thudding. But it's in my head too. This buzzing. This is the booze. Not the zombies. Not the stress. Not the loss.

Oh man, I need this. Gimme a sec.

Oops. That was too much. That gulp made my cheeks go chipmunk.

Must. Slow. Down.

But I can't.

I need this.

I deserve it.

My arm's feeling better already.

# 56
# Topsy-turvy

Telecom handheld transmission:

My feet aren't beneath me. Neither are my legs. Neither is me. I'm just a head floating down the road nearly six feet above the pavement. My head's got a brick in it the size of an anvil and my eyes—all they want is to go to sleep.

No. Not out here. Came too close to being unconscious out in the open before. At least I can remember that much.

Zombies equals bad.

I've looked around, checked things out. I didn't see 'em.

Where am I? How'd I get . . .

Been staring at my feet the whole time I've been walking, well, them and this device. You better be thankful I distracted myself just so you could read this.

I see three of those sentences, not one.

Now I want water.

And bread.

And more Selen—Tequila.

The bottle's empty. It was maybe half-full when I got my hands on it. It was probably too much, half a bottle. I'll probably die of alcohol poisoning instead. Better that than the alternative. Who am I kidding? I'll probably come back anyway and be a nuisance to everyone like usual and, knowing me, a miserable failure of a zombie. Oh, what's that? You want me to eat you? Okay. Then I can't because my stupid hands can't reach the person to grab them. That's all I see in my mind's eye, anyway.

Stop rocking the road!

Carefully, step. Yes, step. One foot in front of the other. Heel toe. Heel toe. I'm probably walking like one of them.

Where am I?

South . . . southwest.

Far from home.

Gone from home.

Selena said she was at home.

I said I was at home.

We said we were at home.

All of us said we were at home.

Her hair is back in my hand, a phantom wig of a girl dead and gone but probably back again out there somewhere.

Alone.

She'll be all right. Even if she's human now she'll die and become one of them again. At least I won't have to kill her this time. Maybe . . . maybe if there's another living soul out there they'll put a bullet between her eyes.

No. Mustn't think of her like that. Not my bab—

There's puke on the keys. I moved the unit out of the way as fast as I could, I swear. Don't get mad.

Ugh. It tastes like sharp, citrusy chicken broth. I hate my guts. My *actual* guts.

Don't you?

You've probably abandoned me by now. Too much talking. Not enough doing. Trust me, I *am* doing something. I'm heading southwest and running out of city. I'll be in the suburbs soon, then the rural areas.

Comptropolis is dead and is kicking me out. Too bad. I kicked it out first.

Stupid city. Stupid life.
Stupid zombies.
I'm going to die.

# 57
# Plastic Bag

Telecom handheld transmission:

Puking didn't help, that is, expel the effects of the alcohol. Not that I mind, but my head is spinning and there's this dull ache behind my eyes. Everything I look at is vibrating. So is my brain. I look to my hand holding Selena's hair and though it is invisible, I can feel every strand.

Southwest.

The city is running out.

*Turn right.* That was not me. That was the hair.

I turn and a giant cement bird greets me, its wings spread out, its sharp beak tilted down as if to peck my face off. Looks like a crow but not as raggedy and it's too majestic to be a pigeon. It takes a minute but my eyes drift past it to a giant sign above the main doors: RAVEN.

Selena could fly away like a bird. I could fix her. She can be restored. That beautiful face, that beautiful body, that beautiful mind. I thought those thoughts once. The gentle weight of the hair begins to lift from my fingers so I make a fist to cling onto it.

I've been here before.

I just don't remember when. Or how. Or why.

In tiny lettering—by comparison—beneath RAVEN it says LABS. What was I doing here? This is a fortress, locked inside and out due to the dangerous toxins and bacteria and diseases they handle. I heard even the staff have to go through a whole procedure coming to and leaving work.

Selena, what have you got to do with this?

The hair is silent. I just hear a buzz in my ears. I need more tequila. No, no that's not the answer yet it seems to have awakened something in me. Is more better? Sometimes less is more. I don't know. I just don't know.

. . .

. . .

. . .

Almost broke the typer this time. Sorry. I threw it on the ground. You might get choppy entries from here on out. Electronics are weird. Nothing but plastic and metal and silicon and somehow it knows how to do things and those things talk to each other.

Talk to each other.

Talking to myself.

No, I talked to Selena. "Make it right," she said. No. No, wait, I said that. I told *me* that.

Make it right.

Raven Labs.

I'm here. This is southwest, almost out of the city. I just don't know what *here* means.

*I want to go home.* Selena's voice.

Say it again, sweetheart. Let me hear you speak. Let me hear the heavenly sound of you saying that. Saying anything.

"Home," she said. I heard it. In my ears. Out loud. But there was no one around me. All I felt in my bunched-up fist was my own skin. The hair was gone. I stretched out my fingers then loosely curled them, hoping to feel those delicate strands laying across my palm again. There was nothing. Just a slight breeze blowing over my skin.

The Raven's doors are mirrored and tinted. I just see

my reflection albeit one in silhouette. Just a mere shadow of myself.

I stare at the guy in the reflection for a good long while. This isn't—*that*—isn't me. My stomach churns, and I throw up to the side. The acidic bite of partially-digested tequila pinches the back of my throat on its way out.

Head still buzzing, I look back at my reflection.

There's a girl standing next to me.

I quickly look to my right where she ought to be. There's no one there. I gaze back at my reflection and it's just me. Then I see her again, as if she's always been there. Her body . . . she's not wearing clothes. She's not naked either. She's got something over her like a gown of some kind or a really wide, long dress. It doesn't sit on her right. Definitely not complimenting or even attractive.

Shut up. Why think like that?

I look to my right again. Whoever this is . . . whoever is in that door's reflection . . . it's not real. She's not real.

Maybe Selena was never real.

Maybe this whole thing with her is made-up?

But how can someone miss something that isn't real? Unless they convince themselves that it is.

The ache behind my eyes quickly turns into a dull pulse, one long drone of pain. I crouch down, thinking maybe that will help. It does. A little. Through teary eyes, I look at the door and see her standing there. I get to my feet knowing full well nobody is beside me. I step closer to the door. The outline of the girl grows larger. So does my own reflection. I step closer again, then one more time. She's wearing what looks like a garbage bag over her head, arms sticking out of holes cut in the sides.

I see you. I see the two of us.

I might lose signal. Be warned.

I go in.

# 58
# Her

Telecom handheld transmission:

"Se-Selena? Is that really you?" I didn't know anymore and, frankly, didn't care. Physical or spiritual or mental, she was there . . . and I was dying.

"Marty." All she had to do was say my name and I knew it was her.

She came closer, hand outstretched. I flinched. The quick flash of the idea of her grabbing me and eating me blitzed across my mind then was gone. Her hand rested on my shoulder. I know that touch. I felt her warmth coming from her palm. Not warmth as in temperature, but warmth that she cared, that she was really here, that she was really *her*.

Tears rolled down my cheeks and I dipped my head.

"Shhh, it's okay," she said softly.

"It's just . . . it's just I've been through so much to get here and . . . and . . ." I sniffled and wiped my eyes. The tears came right back.

"It's okay. I'm here," she said.

I looked up. "Are you?"

I just didn't know anymore.

"I'm real to you, aren't I?"

"Yeah, but are you real-real, like, alive-alive, or is this just some sick game either I'm playing or you're playing or we're playing or . . . I don't know."

There was a moment of a silence before she said, "I'm home, Marty."

I looked around at the barren walls. They were silver. "What? Here?"

All she did was nod.

"I don't understand." I felt her hair in my hand again and thought that when I looked her way she'd be gone.

She wasn't.

"Put that thing away," she said, nodding toward the typing device.

I nodded and shoved it in my pocket.

. . .

. . .

. . .

She'd taken me by the hand. Her skin. Her flesh. All so familiar yet suddenly foreign because the girl I knew kept dying, waking up, dying, waking up—this had to be only temporary.

But I took it. It didn't matter anymore. The wound's gonna kill me. An imaginative Selena or the real deal, what did it matter? I get to see her and touch her before I go.

She led me down a dimly-lit corridor, the light barely reflecting off the silver walls. I didn't want to be here. I wanted to be home, in bed, with her.

Selena didn't say a word as she led me to a pair of large, metal double doors. She slowly let go of my hand.

My eyes were so fixated on the shadow where the doors met that I didn't notice her leaving. She was gone. Her hand in mine . . . gone, too.

I just had her hair and it felt so real in my palm, to the strokes of my fingers. I looked down and saw it. Gorgeous strands of brown ringlets matted in blood.

My hand was on the door handle. I don't remember putting it there. I suppressed the button on top then pulled. It opened and the waft of funk and decay filled my nostrils. Gagging, I coughed hard, felt something rise up in my throat then go back down again.

The alcohol—it hit me. Whatever I threw up wasn't enough. My head spun and I wanted so desperately to close my eyes. Instead, I shuffled into the room, eyes fixed forward, all sound blocked from my ears.

I was wasted.

The hair was as visible as ever in my hand. I didn't care if it was a booze-induced hallucination. This was mine.

Selena was mine!

The thought made a blade pierce my heart and I knew I was wrong. She wasn't mine any more than she was someone else's, no more than she was to herself. I didn't own her. I didn't possess her. She wasn't a part of my life. Not anymore.

Get a grip. Come to terms. Have some peace.

Let her go.

I clung to the air and wandered further in. A sole light source hung from an out-of-date lamp dangling from the ceiling. It shone its glow on the two work tables covered in papers, microscopes, beakers, needles, and a bunch of other tech I didn't know the name for. Contraptions made for what purpose, I didn't know.

Two what looked like showers lay at a forty-five-degree angle across the room. They were domed, the dome covering each from top to bottom.

Electricity mildly buzzed through my brain. My face tingled and my heart finally stopped beating hard.

Booze.

I went up to one of the . . . pods . . . and peered in at the tinted glass.

My heart started slamming again.

It was Selena.

# 59
# First Kill

Telecom handheld transmission:

She lay there like Sleeping Beauty.

I refused to let my eyes fool me yet again into what I was seeing. I moved to the other pod and took a look.

Selena.

Not only did I imagine her before coming into the room, now I'm seeing two of her.

"Marty." I knew that voice.

I turned around and there she was, my Paper Bag Princess, all decked out in a black garbage bag and nothing else.

"Selena, what's going on?"

She didn't reply.

"Selena, I said, 'What's going on?'"

No response.

I stepped closer to her.

Those eyes were chalk-white again, clouded. She was changing again.

"I'm not doing this anymore!" I shouted.

I looked around at the tables and saw a pair of surgical scissors laying toward the corner of one. I grabbed it with the same hand that held the hair. I felt both the metal of the scissors and the coarseness of her dry-bloody hair in my hand. I held both Life and Death and my booze-addled brain pumped power into my system. Not adrenaline. That'd be too easy. This was something else, a sense of rage and inner fortitude.

Selena slowly turned her head toward me and opened her mouth. Nothing but the stench of rotten meat filled the air between us.

"You keep coming back. You keep leaving." My voice rose with every phrase. "You keep giving me hope and you keep taking it away! I'm tired of it! All of it! You! Me! The dead!" I spat on the ground.

She shuffled toward me.

My voice softened. "Selena, don't. No more." I paused. Then, gently, "Okay?"

Her arms were already out. She wanted me.

The tequila told me to move, to get out of the way, to shove her arms aside and run. But there was something else . . . something . . .

The pointy tip of the scissors plowed into the side of Selena's neck, blood gushing out like a geyser.

Black blood.

The blood of the dead.

Her mouth was open and she pushed her head in my direction.

I pulled the scissors from her neck and with each stab back into it shouted, "No! No! No!" With a wild screech, I pulled my arm way back then plunged the scissors into Selena's temple. Black blood ran out and I used all my drunken strength to push the blades in as far as possible.

She stumbled to the side then folded at the knees. She tried to stand and a piece of me wanted to help her up. I reached out and with two hands she grabbed mine and started biting my fingers. I yanked my bleeding hand away, put a palm to her forehead and shoved her head back, giving me enough time to yank out the scissors.

Like a wild man, I brought the scissors down on the top of her head with everything I had. I pulled the blades out and did it again, each time slamming the instrument into her skull harder and harder. Was I talking? Screaming? Crying? I didn't know. Just dizzy and spinny from the booze, nothing but power and rage pumping through every single cell in my body.

Each pull of the blade pulled up chunks of flesh and meat. The blood shot out at first then eventually slowed to a bubbling pool that ran over the top of her head and down all sides like a stringy wig.

Those white eyes didn't care. There was no flinching, no expressions of pain. Just a slack jaw with jagged-edged teeth.

I toppled onto her and pulled the scissors out and brought them back into her face. I hammered down on her with those blades until my inner clock told me it'd been thirty seconds of it. A minute. Two minutes. An hour.

I glanced at the pods. I glanced at her body and the remnants of her head.

What have I done?

I fell over to the side and just lay there, my eyes carefully looking at Selena for any sign of movement.

Zombies in the hall. Their groans. Some footfalls. Good thing the door to this room was closed. Hopefully they'll pass by and that'll it be it in regards to them.

Where did the scissors go? I looked around myself, thinking I might have dropped them on the floor. No scissors. No weapons. Nothing to—

My fingers found metal and with a sigh of relief, I went to bring my hand before my eyes to see the blades and take some sort of comfort in them. But they were heavy. I lifted the metal and squinted in the dim light.

A dented toaster stared back at me, smeared with blood and dried chunks of skin and flesh.

I fell backward, the dizziness from the booze and

exertion getting to me.

It was me, wasn't it?

The toaster. The hair.

I still felt the toaster in my hand. I shook it off like mud. It didn't make a sound after I cast it away. Just another thing from my imagination. But Selena's body was still there, the scissors on the floor between us.

I looked at the pods.

It was hard to tell from this distance, but I'm pretty sure I still saw a Selena in each one.

Back to the floor, back to the girl laying there with no face and covered in nothing but gore and stringy flesh, running with shine as each trickle rolled down the tops of her ears, inside the crevices, and finally dripping off the earlobe to the floor.

It was me.

I was the killer.

I killed my girl.

I just didn't know if she was dead when I did.

# 60
# Two

Telecom handheld transmission:

Arm throbbing, I dragged myself across the floor. I'm holding the typing device now, just for you. If I croak on my way to the pods, at least you'll know I went out trying to reach you and tell you my story.

Each movement forward took forever or at least felt like it. The pods were getting closer. I looked over my shoulder and Selena still lay dead on the floor. There was no indication she would get up and come after me.

All went dark for a second. Or maybe a minute. Truth is, I don't know how long I was out for. Hopefully only a couple minutes. Maybe five. Whatever.

When I got to the pods, my hand tried to find purchase on their smooth domes to help myself up, but instead my fingers ran down the plasti-glass, a layer of blood between my skin and the pod's covering.

The hair was gone from my hand and I didn't think it was coming back. It didn't need to. I knew what it was and it wasn't hair.

It was flesh. Thin ropes of flesh that I pretended was hair when I came here that day after killing Selena for the first time. I must have been drunk because I don't remember much. There was me, the gore I held, the zombies on the streets. The running. The stopping. The hiding. I didn't have to fight that day. What mattered most was getting Selena's DNA to Raven. Yet I was right when I arrived. The whole place was abandoned. I came into *this* room. I needed a doctor. A scientist. A nurse. Somebody who knew something about blood and DNA and, if rumor was right, cloning.

There was nothing. Nobody. Just an empty room.

Not to cheap out on you, but I truly don't remember much. Something about standing there a long time. Standing *here* before the once-empty pods. I looked them over. At the time, I didn't realize they were connected by three thick metal tubes about a foot long, uniting the two pods like a married couple. What was in there? Wires? Those wouldn't be protected with metal.

Unless they were important.

Maybe tubes? Those can be delicate.

But somehow those pipes made sense. Somehow I knew that's why there were two Selenas in front of me and one dead behind me, and I lost count of how many others strewn about the city.

I wanted the original.

I wanted the girl in my kitchen before I hit her with the toaster. I wanted the girl on my couch before her eyes went white.

I wanted what was *before*.

I wanted Life.

And all I got was death.

My legs barely held me up as I stood before the two pods. I gripped one where the plasti-glass met the metal of the pod itself. Pulling, pushing, slamming the side of my fist against it. Why won't you open!

What sounded like an old-fashioned squeegee came from inside one of the pods—hands sliding against glass.

The pod opened, the dome-like covering swinging wide like a door. Selena's eyes were open. I scanned them for whiteness. She looked at me and gently smiled, her brown eyes shimmering with what I supposed were happy tears.

"M-Marty?"

"Selena," I said.

"Help me . . ." She leaned forward. I pulled on her arm to help her straighten.

"Did it work?" she asked.

"Did what work?" I replied.

Then I realized she didn't really ask me that. She had said, "What have you done?" Her eyes were on the body on the floor. My heart broke at the prospect that she thought it was me who killed the other her. If she knew it was another her, that was. But the heartache was unwarranted and it was just me feeling sorry for myself. Just me appalled at what I'd become. I shook my head, hoping to shake away the alcoholic haze.

It didn't work.

"Are you . . . are you all right?" I asked.

Her eyes were on the other pod. She slowly approached it and peered inside. She stepped back with a gasp and a hand over her mouth.

"What have you done!" she screamed at me.

Silence. It was all I had.

"You bastard!" she said, laying both fists into me, pounding away at my chest as if at a nail that just wouldn't sink in.

The hair. Raven. No, not hair. Flesh. In my daze that day I did something. Didn't know what I was doing but I did something.

Selena yanked the other pod open.

"How'd you—" I started but her ice-cold stare shut me up.

She stood there looking at herself, this time both hands covering her mouth. She shook her head slowly side to side. When she looked at me—I've never seen that look in her eyes before. It was different and not *undead* different either.

It was dismay.

She pulled her hands away from her mouth. "What did you do?"

"I don't remember. Pieces . . . I remember pieces."

"Obviously you did *something*."

Glancing down at my feet, I straightened my head when the weight of the dizziness took over. I was so tired. So, so tired.

No more of this.

The Selena in the pod opened her eyes. Alive. Well. Healthy.

The Selena I was just talking to stepped further away as the other climbed out. The other stumbled but then steadied her footing.

"This can't be happening . . ." I breathed.

My arm.

Fog over my eyes.

# 61
# Last Call

Telecom handheld transmission:

My elbows hit the floor hard, a jolt of pain rocking the underside of my forearms from the impact. My neck hurt, but I suppose that was from tensing it before I hit the ground in order to save the back of my head from smacking the floor.

Both Selenas loomed over me. They kept staring at each other and rightly so. Anyone would stare if they saw themselves looking right back at them in the flesh.

"Selena," I whispered. "I'm really tired. I need help." My eyes closed involuntarily. The sweetness of sleep quickly began to overtake me. I forced my eyes open as wide as they would go in an effort to stay awake.

Jay's bandage was soaked in blood now.

I thought I heard movement from somewhere above—behind—my head. The girl on the floor. Was she coming over? I waited. And waited. My temples anticipated the grip of clawing fingers as the dead woman would take hold of my skull and bite into it. But she never came.

And only one Selena was by my side.

"Where—" I started.

"Gone," was all she said.

"She's going to . . . going to . . ."

"Going to what? Marty, where are we? Why did you bring me here? Why was I in that thing?"

In that *thing*.

The pod.

The memory came in pulses.

I threw the flesh into one of the pods and closed its door. I flicked on every switch I saw, pressed every button. Went to the tables and grabbed beakers and bottles and splashed every color of liquid rainbow against the pod, thinking somehow I was baptizing it in a mix of stuff that would bring her back. It was stupid. It did nothing in hindsight.

But the pod did do something.

It created Selena.

The horrifying thought of the Selena I killed with the toaster being the real one and not a clone . . . . Tears rolled out the corners of my eyes.

The fog increased and speaking was growing difficult.

"I-I can't see you," I said.

She held my hand in hers and drew in close. "I'm here, Marty. I don't know what you did or . . ."

"Why am I on the floor?" The last question took all my wind.

She only nodded.

After taking a deep breath, I said, "Don't go outside. Stay. Here. With me." I couldn't tell her what awaited her as much as I wanted to prepare her. This Selena was going to turn too at some point and soon she'd be walking amongst the dead, and soon after that, nothing more than a decaying face blended into a sea of monsters.

"Let me . . ." Why wouldn't the words come?

"What?" she said softly.

My hand was partly in my pocket but I didn't have the strength to dig it all the way in and—

"Here," she said and fished out the typing device.

She took both my hands and locked them around the device. "Finish whatever you started."

I wish I could say I started a revolution or some kind of war against the dead. I wish I could say I wasn't a drunk screw-up with more issues than can be counted.

I wish I wasn't a killer. There's a place in hell for people like me.

Hell came to Earth here in Comptropolis. Maybe we were already in it. Maybe this is Hell.

Maybe you're in it too.

Maybe . . .

I'm looking through powdered glass.

I can't see the keys.

I can't see anything.

My words are my voice.

Selena will turn but I will turn first.

I'm sorry, reader. Thought I'd make more of a difference.

I have to go. Wish I had tequila so I could finish this the way I started but, I suppose, I'm drunk already and was drunk when I first said hi to you.

Good enough.

Good . . . enough.

Welcome to Zomtropolis.

# About the Author

A.P. Fuchs is the author of over 40 books and the writer-artist of multiple comics. He's been writing and publishing for over 20 years and doesn't plan to stop any time soon. When he's not writing, he indulges in video creation and visiting the toy store for collectibles and superhero memorabilia.

A.P. Fuchs makes his home in Winnipeg, Manitoba, right in the middle of North America (no, really, go look at a map).

His official website is CanisterX.com

# ALSO BY A.P. FUCHS

## BLOOD OF MY WORLD TRILOGY

DISCOVERY OF DEATH
MEMORIES OF DEATH
LIFE OF DEATH

## UNDEAD WORLD TRILOGY

BLOOD OF THE DEAD
POSSESSION OF THE DEAD
REDEMPTION OF THE DEAD

## THE AXIOM-MAN™ SAGA
(LISTED IN READING ORDER)

AXIOM-MAN or
AXIOM-MAN: TENTH YEAR ANNIVERSARY
SPECIAL EDITION
EPISODE NO. 0: FIRST NIGHT OUT
DOORWAY OF DARKNESS
EPISODE NO. 1: THE DEAD LAND
CITY OF RUIN
EPISODE NO. 2: UNDERGROUND CRUSADE
OUTLAW
EPISODE NO. 3: RUMBLINGS
FROZEN STORM (SIDE ADVENTURE)
OF MAGIC AND MEN (COMIC BOOK)

## MECH APOCALYPSE

MECH APOCALYPSE

# OTHER FICTION

A Stranger Dead
A Red Dark Night
April (writing as Peter Fox)
Magic Man (deluxe chapbook)
The Way of the Fog (The Ark of Light Vol. 1)
Devil's Playground (with Keith Gouveia)
On Hell's Wings (with Keith Gouveia)
Zombie Fight Night: Battles of the Dead
Magic Man Plus 15 Tales of Terror
Undeniable
The Dance of Mervo and Father Clown
Flash Attack: Thrilling Stories of Terror, Adventure, and Intrigue
Giganti-gator Death Machine: Triple Feature

# ANTHOLOGIES (AS EDITOR)

Dead Science
Elements of the Fantastic
Vicious Verses and Reanimated Rhymes: Zany Zombie
Poetry for the Undead Head
Metahumans vs the Undead
Bigfoot Terror Tales Vol. 1 (with Eric S. Brown)
Bigfoot Terror Tales Vol. 2 (with Eric S. Brown)
Metahumans vs Werewolves

## NON-FICTION

BOOK MARKETING FOR THE
FINANCIALLY-CHALLENGED AUTHOR
CANADIAN SCRIBBLER: COLLECTED LETTERS OF AN
UNDERGROUND WRITER
LOOK, UP ON THE SCREEN! THE BIG BOOK OF
SUPERHERO MOVIE REVIEWS
GETTING DOWN AND DIGITAL: HOW TO SELF-PUBLISH YOUR
BOOK
THE CANISTER X TRANSMISSION: YEAR ONE
THE CANISTER X TRANSMISSION: YEAR TWO
THE CANISTER X TRANSMISSION: YEAR THREE
THE CANISTER X TRANSMISSION: YEAR FOUR
THE CANISTER X TRANSMISSION: THE LONG YEAR FIVE

## POETRY

THE HAND I'VE BEEN DEALT
HAUNTED MELODIES AND OTHER DARK POEMS
STILL ABOUT A GIRL

**WWW.CANISTERX.COM**